PIPER PAN AND HER MERRY BAND: BOOK ONE

Always believe in your dreams!

Lindy MacLaine

The Curse of
the Neverland

Lindy MacLaine

SOARING BOOKS PRESS

Sequim, Washington

Soaring Books Press
P.O. Box 1592
Sequim, Washington 98382

Publisher's Note: This is a work of fiction. Names, characters, places and incidents are a product of the author's imagination. Locales and public names are sometimes used for atmospheric purposes. Any resemblance to actual people, living or dead, or to businesses, companies, events, institutions or locales is completely coincidental.

Published by Soaring Books Press
Edited by Celeste Bennett, www.BennettHastings.com
Cover Design by Marjorie Schoelles, www.MermaidSand.com
Cover Art and Illustrations by Aisha Zaleha Latip

The Curse of the Neverland/Lindy MacLaine – 2nd edition
Published 12/15
ISBN 978-0-9969906-0-8

Published in the United States of America

For all those who've loved the Neverland
and who long for adventures that matter.

CONTENTS

"Piper. Piper Pizzinni. You can call me Pip."

A Glimpse Ahead

"**H**ow long will it take to get to the Neverland?" Pip craned her neck to peer up at the elderly fairy hauling her by the belt loop. Heck, for all she knew, maybe it was her fairy godmother. Great, *great* fairy godmother, she thought.

"That depends on you." The ancient pixie's voice, strained with effort, shimmered through the chilly night air.

Second star to the right and straight on 'til morning. The directions rang in Pip's mind. She'd seen the play *Peter Pan* on stage so many times she practically knew the lines by heart. Her father had designed sets for more than one production, and she'd watched rehearsal after rehearsal of her mother teaching swordplay.

Piper gulped. The memory both thrilled and threatened. She'd always hoped she'd get to the Neverland. But after her parents were stolen, she'd been afraid to think much about the magical place for fear something else bad would happen. The long-remembered image of the dragon-borne pirate ship framed against the full moon over the Space Needle had haunted her for five years. Now, here she was on her eleventh birthday, if it could possibly be believed, sailing through the air toward the Neverland, butt-first.

All condo units in Fairyland's Crystal City came with the required portrait of the fairy king and queen.

Royal Intervention

Public declarations and courtly commands have their place, but the real decisions in the fairy kingdom happen at teatime in the palace sunroom.

"If we do not take action soon, my queen," said King Oberon, sipping his Earl Grey tea from a porcelain cup, "The Neverland will meet its final end and fade fore'er from our magical realm."

"And what, pray tell, do you suggest, my dear?" Queen Titania peered over her rhinestone-studded reading glasses at her husband, laying her newspaper aside. "We're bound by the laws of free will, you know."

The king of the fairies nabbed an extra piece of candied ginger and popped it into his mouth. "Free will, dung hill," he said.

Titania raised a regal eyebrow. "Language, darling, really!"

"The fools have gone too far," Oberon said. He raised a hand in acknowledgement. "I grant you this:

5

overt action is not the path to take. But nothing says we cannot *lean*."

The queen held his gaze. Her shoulders slumped a smidgeon. Her wings drooped. "That's true, it's now or never," she said. A moment more and she straightened, lifting her teacup in a salute. "Perhaps, my king, we'll lean. Just a bit."

†

"Good Morning, Belle, formerly Tinker Bell!"

Belle burrowed her head into her feather pillow, willing the regal wake-up call away. Why wouldn't they give it up? She hadn't gotten out of bed in two days.

All condo units in Fairyland's Crystal City came with the required portrait of the fairy king and queen. Belle hadn't realized when she moved in—how long ago? Was it months? Years? —that it talked. Daily.

"Good morning, good morning!" the king sang. "It's great to stay up late, good morning, good morning, to you!"

"Nnngg," Belle covered her ears and pulled her duvet over her head. She just couldn't see the point in getting up. Come to think of it, she hadn't seen much point in anything lately.

"Belle, formerly of the magical isle, 'tis time to

join in Tai Chi on the quad." Queen Titania's voice was much harder to ignore.

Belle attempted to sit up, her old bones protesting. "Yes, Your Highnesses." Gravity won, and she fell back into the warm cocoon of her four-poster bed. "Right away, Your Highnesses." Surely they'd go bother some other poor fairy in a minute.

"If you'll not join the others for Tai Chi, at least meditate right here in your room," said King Oberon.

"Don't coddle her, dear," said the queen. "Belle, you will begin on the count of three. If not, you shall know our wrath. One … Two … Three."

No help for it. She was going to have to move. With a monumental effort, Belle slid out of bed. She crumpled into a half-lotus on the plush beige carpet, her back propped against the bed frame. "All right, all right, I'm here," she mumbled. The chilly morning air raised gooseflesh on her arms. Her ivory silk nightgown was all beauty and no warmth.

"Allow me," said the king from his portrait. Merry flames filled the nearby fireplace. "An older fairy like you deserves to be waited on, 'tis not so?"

Belle bristled. It was true she'd seen more years than she cared to count. If she'd remained ever young, as she had during her days with Peter Pan, it wouldn't matter. But since he'd left the Neverland,

and since—well, that other thing—she knew she showed at least seventy years of her age. Still. No one had a right to point that out to a lady!

"Hmmm," Belle managed. The warmth from the fire relaxed her. If she just closed her eyes and pretended to meditate, maybe she could sleep a little longer. Belle rested her hands in her lap, palms up, middle fingers touching thumbs, and took three deep breaths.

"That's very good, Belle," called the queen. "And thus it begins."

Belle began sinking through gray layers in her mind. She'd pretend to meditate and, instead, have a little nap. Sliding toward sleep, she thought she heard the queen speak again, as though from a long way away.

"Pray do not lean too hard, my gentle king."

The visions came fast and furious behind Belle's eyelids, with crystalline clarity. She stiffened, as if connected to an electric current. There was Peter, in all his youthful glory.

"Oh, Peter," Belle sighed. "Why did you ever have to leave?"

The youth in her mind folded his arms in that know-it-all way of his, turned on his heel, and disappeared. Belle watched, as if through thick glass, as Peter took the hand of a smiling, blonde girl. She was one in the long line of Spring Cleaning girls. That one was called Isabelle. Belle winced. She still couldn't believe Peter had left the Neverland to grow up with her. Just because the girl had been clever enough to tell Peter he was too "cowardly custard" to grow up, he'd had to go and prove her wrong. And to think her name ended in "belle"! Irritation twisted in Belle's stomach.

In a flash, Peter and the girl were grown, dressed in wedding regalia, walking down the aisle. Peter looked so handsome in his tuxedo! He leaned in to give his bride one of those thimble-things with his lips. Belle squeezed her eyes tighter. She didn't want to watch Peter love someone else.

Before Belle could break this strange parade of visions, Peter aged. Strands of gray wove through his red-brown wavy hair. The bride on his arm wasn't his wife-to-be anymore; it was Peter's daughter, Angela, with auburn hair tumbling to her waist. He was giving her away in marriage to a dark-haired, dark-eyed, man. A tear rolled down Peter's cheek as he watched Angela say, "I do."

The scene shifted again. Peter sat behind the steering wheel of a car, windshield running thick with rain, wipers unable to keep up with the torrent.

"Look out, Peter!" a woman's voice cried. Belle didn't know if the voice was hers or Isabelle's. Their screams wove together, shrilling as the headlights of a truck plowed straight into the car. Everything went dark. Belle didn't want to see any more.

It didn't seem to matter what Belle wanted. A wooded cemetery appeared. Peter's daughter, Angela, stood with her husband, their babe in his arms. Angela laid a bouquet of flowers at the base of two headstones.

"Mom, Dad," Angela said, her voice unsteady. "This is our daughter, your granddaughter. Her name is Piper. I wish you could have met her."

Belle felt tears streaming down her cheeks. Her heart hurt. Her breath came in hiccupping gasps. Again, before she could break away from the picture in her head, it changed.

Belle felt light, as a fairy ought to feel. She was sitting on the softest of clouds, looking down at her emerald green magical isle. Her heart bumped, the ache now one of longing. *The Neverland. Home.* The sea sparkled in the sunlight. The mountain peaks glimmered white. There was Kidd's Cove, the *Jolly Roger*'s sails fluttering in the breeze. She imagined she could see her pirate protégé, Captain Li'l Jack, standing at the helm, bellowing orders at his crew.

Belle's breathing slowed and her lips curved in a smile. It was all right. No matter what else had happened, the Neverland was there, comforting her, beckoning her.

But it wasn't all right. The scene mutated, like the edges of a burning letter. The island blackened. Trees stood barren. Vegetation gave way to sand, and all signs of life disappeared. Fear stabbed at Belle's heart. Had the fairy Pearl been right all along? Had the enchantment become the Neverland's curse?

The image of Captain Li'l Jack filled Belle's mind. "I'll not stop 'til I have enough," he roared. His once-blonde hair and goatee had streaks of silver now, but his features were as handsome as ever. His blue eyes flashed, and he gripped the silver vial that he wore on a chain around his neck, with both hook and claw. "I've almost enough to grow real hands." He held up his metal appendages, clearly imagining ten digits, whole and sound. Belle could feel his yearning, a force that threatened to crack her chest open.

Then it seemed to Belle he was looking straight at her, a snarl on his pretty face. "I don't care what promises I made, Belle. I'll feed the dragon the whole human race if necessary! Who needs you or yer blasted magical island?"

Belle's heart hammered as if the threat were imminent. Anger rolled through her, and she longed to flail at him with her fists. But all she could do was watch.

Li'l Jack sent his First Mate, Flea, up the rigging with two lanterns, glowing red. Standing at the ship's prow, Li'l Jack shouted skyward. "'Tis time to hunt, me dragon!"

An enormous black beast appeared above the ship, eyes whirling red, powerful wings blocking the sky. Lightning cracked and thunder shook. The dragon arced into the cove, and its bulk submerged in the dark, roiling waves. Breaking the surface with a roar, it coiled its massive body about the *Jolly Roger*. Mighty wings beating, it launched into the sky, bearing the pirate ship with it.

The image faded to black. Belle waited for more, but the movie playing in her head seemed to have finished. She used her fingers to peel her eyelids open and looked around. She still sat, leaning against her bed, in her elegant beige condo in Fairyland's Crystal City. Trembling with recognition of the truth, she rose, wobbling, to her feet. The fog that had surrounded her for weeks had lifted. She dressed and gathered a few things, moving more quickly and easily as she went.

Ready at last, she addressed the portraits. "Your Majesties, I've got to go."

"Oh?" The queen raised an eyebrow.

Belle narrowed her eyes. No one took that tone with her. "Yes. I have an heir to fetch," she snapped. "Peter Pan's granddaughter may be just a girl, but she's the only chance the Neverland's got." With that, Belle blinked twice and disappeared into thin air.

The king and queen looked at each other and smiled.

"How was that for a lean, my sweetest queen?" Oberon asked.

Titania's eyes twinkled. "'Twas subtle, and perfectly aimed, my king," she said. "I could not have done it better myself."

"High praise indeed," said the king.

Fitch's Last Ditch Foster Home

"Piper, meet your new foster mother, Mrs. Fitch."

Piper Pizzinni tried to smile. The lady wore a bathrobe and had curlers in her hair. Not a good sign, considering it was the middle of the afternoon on a gray Seattle Saturday.

"I'll leave you to get settled in, Piper." Miss Henning had been Piper's caseworker for the last five years, since her parents disappeared. She wasn't friendly, but at least she was familiar.

"Thanks, Miss Henning," Piper mumbled, watching her only stability walk away toward the official Child Protection Services vehicle parked at the curb. Piper gripped her small suitcase and stepped into the dingy house, ignoring her rising sense of panic.

"The girls call this 'Fitch's Last Ditch Foster Home.'" Mrs. Fitch blocked her way, arms crossed and lips tight. "If you're here, it's because no one else will take you."

Piper resisted the urge to flinch under the hateful

gaze. "It's nice of you to take me in," she lied. "I'm sure we'll get along just fine."

"We'll see about that." Mrs. Fitch turned on her heel and beckoned Piper to follow.

Piper climbed the stairs, keeping her distance from the swaying pink bathrobe. The woman wore enough perfume to offend a skunk. The carpet runner under Piper's feet was threadbare, the exposed wood at the edges chipped and dirty.

"Hurry up!" As they reached the upper landing, Mrs. Fitch reached down and yanked Piper by the upper arm, pinching as she did so. Piper winced. She'd have a bruise, but she'd had worse.

"Down the hall to the left. You'll meet the rest of the girls."

Piper turned into the indicated doorway. A large bare room, each wall hosting a metal bunk bed, met her gaze. No bars on the window, but it felt like a prison cell. Piper shuddered. She counted seven girls, like planets in a solar system. It felt lonely in here, each girl in her own orbit, barely aware of the others. But all seven stopped what they were doing and stared at her.

"Girls, this is Piper," Mrs. Fitch said. Piper held herself rigid as the woman stepped into the room behind her. "She'll sleep in Sally's bunk." The sad excuse for a foster mother wheeled back out into the hallway, her voice lashing back. "I don't want to hear from any of you until I call you down for supper."

"Hi," Piper said to the room in general, forcing a grin. Wrong choice. Six pairs of eyes narrowed at her. The seventh's eyes widened, then burst into tears. Piper guessed that one was maybe three years old.

"Now look what you've done!" growled a pasty redheaded girl with freckles.

Piper shrugged. "Just trying to be friendly."

"Give it a rest before you do any more damage," the girl said. Her voice was as big as her body.

"How many foster girls does it take to change a light bulb?" Piper quipped. Surprise and puzzlement looked back at her. At least she'd managed to throw them off their game.

"I dodn't doe, how bany?" A runny-nosed, stringy-blonde-haired little girl asked.

"That depends," Piper said.

The redhead raised an eyebrow and looked menacing.

"It only takes one foster girl," Piper said hastily, "but it takes a whole caboodle of adults to tell her how to do it."

The blonde giggled and snorted. "Dat's fuddy," she said. She wiped her nose on the back of her sleeve. "I'b Stingky," she offered. "Dice to beet you."

"Huh," the redhead said. "Not bad." She looked at Piper grudgingly for a moment longer, and then relented. "Okay. We're the Lifers. You know, foster kids for life, get it?" She gave Piper a look that said if she didn't, she'd get a fist in the face.

"I get it," Piper said.

"Good." The redhead nodded. "I'm Pudge, I'm twelve. Zonker is the one who looks comatose over there. Zonk for short. She's eleven." Pudge gestured to a tall, dark girl lying prone on one of the bottom bunks.

"Midge is the Samurai brainiac. She's nine." A girl all in black, wearing glasses, gave Pudge a dirty look from her top bunk. She glanced at Piper before leaning back over her book. Her long, shiny black hair swung like a curtain over her face.

"You just met Stinky," Pudge indicated the blonde. "She's seven." Next, she pointed at another top bunk. Twin girls, identical from their quirky half-smiles to their dark brown bowl-haircuts poked each other and giggled. "That's Flim and Flam." The girls in question weren't watching. Obviously, what they were doing was far more interesting. "They're six," Pudge continued. "They speak Spanish most of the time, but don't let 'em fool you. They understand English just fine."

Pudge pointed to the smallest girl, whose cries

had turned to hiccups, her thumb firmly planted in her mouth. "Thumb is four, even though she looks and acts like she's two." The little girl's long-lashed brown eyes crinkled in a smile, and her chocolate-brown cheeks dimpled, surprising Piper.

"Hello, there," Piper smiled back, this time for real.

In all the foster homes Piper had been in, there had never been other foster girls. She'd always been the family add-on who didn't measure up.

Friends. Piper barely allowed the word in her mind, flattening the whisper of hope before it could take root. Heck, the only friends she'd made in five years were the employees at the Nickelodeon, where she unofficially did chores so they'd let her sit and watch movies for hours. Who did she think she was, dreaming that it might be possible to have real friends? In a place like this, everyone was probably too busy fighting over a full serving of dinner to care about each other.

"Which one was Sally's bunk?" Piper asked.

The smile slid off the big redhead's face, and the whole room got quiet. Pudge's thumb jerked toward the bunk under the twins. At least it was the wall with the window.

Piper pushed her suitcase under the bed. She saw a rope ladder, piled in a heap on the floor, attached to the metal frame at one end. "Fire escape ladder?" she asked, standing back up.

"Uh huh," Pudge said. "Fitch was supposed to have a fire escape installed. Cheap old bag." She laughed, a booming noise that startled Piper. "It works good for sneakin' out, though, if you're willin' t' pay the price."

"Bad?"

"Bad enough," the braniac girl said, without looking up from her book. "Really not worth it."

We'll see about that, Piper thought. She planned on slipping out a little later tonight. The access couldn't be better. She would pretend to feel sick. When everyone else went down to dinner, out the window she'd go, easy as pie.

Piper shrugged off her army surplus backpack before sitting on the bed. She bounced up and down on the bunk experimentally, and decided to take another risk. "So what happened to Sally? Did she die, or what?"

Nobody answered, each girl suddenly consumed with what she was doing. Piper stopped bouncing and stared around the room, from one averted face to the next.

Finally, the one she thought had been asleep turned her head toward Piper. To Piper, she looked like an exotic queen. High cheekbones, gorgeous bronze skin, face framed by two long braids. Zonk's voice was low and smooth, in contrast with the bitter look on her face. "She was adopted."

Nothing more had to be said. If Piper had nothing else in common with this multi-colored group of rag-tag girls, she shared the jagged pain of being unwanted.

For the moment, they were united. But Piper knew it wouldn't last long. Once they learned what she was determined to do, they would think she was crazy, a loser, an idiot, and so on. It had happened to her in every foster home so far—how many now? Ten? Eleven? It had been five years since her parents' disappearance. Five years—each of them worse than the last.

The other girls might be able to respect Piper's sworn oath to someday, somehow, go where her parents had gone and rescue them. But the whole truth was just too hard to believe. So she mostly kept the details to herself. The fact was, her parents had been captured by a pirate captain and flown off in a ship carried through the sky by a dragon. Crazy as it was, Piper knew beyond a shadow of a doubt that they'd been taken to the Neverland.

"Wha' d' ya say your name was?" Pudge's loud voice interrupted Piper's reverie.

Her heart sank at the scorn on Pudge's face.

Here we go, she thought. She answered as easily as she could. "Piper. Piper Pizzinni. You can call me Pip." She'd never given anyone the option of calling her Pip before. That was what her parents had called her.

"Piper." Pudge's lip curled. "Yeah, I've heard about you. You're the one who keeps getting caught trying to do a Peter Pan from high places."

Piper looked back at Pudge and willed her face to stay blank.

"How dumb can you get?" Pudge went on. "If you want to off yourself, there are lots of easier ways. My aunt used pills. Zonk's mother just drank herself to death."

"Shut ... up." Zonk didn't move, didn't open her eyes, but her voice cut the air like glass shards. Piper noted with satisfaction that it wiped the grin right off Pudge's face. Unfortunately, it also layered mean onto the scorn.

"Just sayin'," Pudge said to Zonk before turning on Piper. "Nah. I don't think we'll bother calling you Pip." She leered. "We'll just call you *Pipsqueak*."

Piper scanned the other faces in the room. Except for Zonk's, they mirrored Pudge's. They liked having someone new at the bottom of the heap. She shrugged. "Fine," she said. "Whatever." She lay back on the bed, ignoring the jeering laughter.

Forget what she'd hoped about these girls becoming friends. She didn't need them. She didn't need anyone. She'd find her way to the Neverland on her own. In her mind, she flew through clouds, letting the soft moisture cool her burning cheeks.

CHAPTER TWO

The Painful Truth

L eaving the Fairy Kingdom to its dreary business, Belle blinked twice and ended her self-imposed exile. She had said she'd go find Peter's heir right away. But what was the hurry? She'd ignored the girl this long, what would a little more time hurt? The siren call of home vibrated in her bones. Choosing her destination, she willed herself high over the magical island.

She burst from darkness into light. The Neverland! At last! She took a deep breath to prepare for her descent, and promptly choked in dismay. Senses assaulted, she froze mid-dive. Smoky air clung, sticky on her wings. The reek of charred wood and sulfur burned her nose and planted a bitter taste in her mouth. Looking down, her eyes met a nightmare sight. "Oh, no!" she croaked. Apparently the vision she'd had during her meditation had been spot on.

The Neverland's familiar curves and ridges should have been fringed with green, crowned by ancient forests, its shores ringed by turquoise water.

Instead it looked like something dead flung into a mud puddle.

Trembling began in the tips of Belle's wings and spread to her heart. "Shivering snails!" she whispered. "How long have I been gone?" Time in the Fairy Kingdom passed so slowly as to hardly matter. But any amount of time might have gone by in the Neverland while she'd sulked in the Crystal City.

Fury simmered in her belly and her cheeks burned. "Sheer stupidity," she muttered. "I thought he'd miss me so much he'd change his ways!" She hugged herself to quiet her shivers. Obviously, Captain Li'l Jack and his precious black dragon, Sincoraz, had been having a field day in her absence.

One thing was clear. The Neverland *had* to be saved. But not by a small female relative of Peter's. She'd do it herself. Covering her nose and mouth with her hands, Belle dropped straight for Kidd's Cove. The *Jolly Roger* would be anchored there. The pirate captain had some explaining to do.

She could have found Li'l Jack's porthole in her sleep. After all, she'd practically lived there in the years after Peter Pan left. She peered through the thick wavy glass, eyes watering. Sure enough, Captain Li'l Jack was in.

He stood, squinting at a silver vial hung from

a chain around his neck. Belle shivered. The image echoed her meditation with disturbing accuracy. He clutched the vial with the bare metal claw that stood in for his right hand.

A lacey white sleeve draped the claw, but she'd seen him without long sleeves many years ago when he'd been a boy. His own right arm ended just below the elbow in a nasty nub. Two metal bars completed his forearm and became pincers. His left arm grew longer, almost to where the hand should be, before it ended in an ugly scar. A metal hook capped the wrist instead of a hand.

Glancing up, he spotted her. His lip twitched, and his moustache jumped.

She watched as he unlatched the porthole with his hook. It was JAS Hook's very hook—Li'l Jack had been awarded the famous appendage when he'd become Captain of the *Jolly Roger*. It was much shinier and sharper than the hook he'd arrived with.

Li'l Jack beamed a toothy grin.

Belle knew better than to fall for that smile of his.

Belle took a deep breath. *Remember what you came for*, she told herself. Aloud, she said, "Is that what I think it is?" She pointed to the vial, still clutched in Li'l Jack's claw. If it was, she understood completely what was wrong here. The life had literally been sucked out of the Neverland by that horrible black dragon, Sincoraz.

"The very same. Sincoraz's Elixir of Life. Liquid gold," he chortled. "Soon I'll have enough to use on meself—to grow *real hands*."

Belle lost her barely-held composure. "I can't believe you would exchange the Neverland for hands!" she shrilled.

"Me hands are me life dream," he snarled. "The chance to be whole is worth much more than a silly island and a stupid old fairy godmother."

Belle gasped. "Stupid? Old? Everything you enjoy is because of me. Give me my due respect, young man."

Li'l Jack gave a sharp bark of laughter. "Young man? Take another look, granny." The look he tossed her added insult to injury. "I'm not yer little adopted Pan-replacement anymore. I haven't needed ye for years." His voice calmed. "Besides, ye've been at sea five years yerself. What course did ye sail, anyway?"

"Five years?" Shock filled Belle's head like a balloon inflating. She sank to the plush red arm of Jack's chair, thudding to a seat. "I've been gone five years?" she repeated. "It's been that long since we argued?"

"Oh, aye. 'Twas five years ago I captured Peter

Pan's grown daughter and her fool of a husband."
The words clearly tasted sweet.

"And fed them to Sincoraz." Belle shuddered.
"You promised not to go on collecting humans for
dragon fodder! You said you'd let things return to
their natural order."

The captain cocked his head. "Perhaps I did."
He shrugged. "And so I will, after I have me hands.
Which I haven't. Not quite." He lifted the vial to his
ear and shook it gently.

"If you let it go on any longer, the Neverland
will die!" She must make him understand. "*You* let
Sincoraz strip it of life. *You're* the one responsible for
this." Her anger turned to fear and she felt suddenly
weak. With a wave of dread, she knew. Her own
fate was linked to the Neverland's. If she stayed
here, and the Neverland died, so would she. Her
vision blurred and she felt faint. This was horrible.
It seemed she *couldn't* save her home, and this—this
powerful protégé of hers, *wouldn't*.

Captain Li'l Jack watched her with a shrewd smile.
"Perhaps I am responsible." He shrugged again.
"When one wants something, there are sacrifices to
be made."

Gathering her forces, Belle flew at Li'l Jack's face,
stopping inches before his eyes. "Sacrifices?" she
fumed. "But who's had to sacrifice? Not you!"

She didn't know why she didn't stop talking right there. If she'd had any sense at all, she would have kept her cards close to her chest. It seemed she couldn't help herself. "Oh," she chuckled, "but you'll get yours, Li'l Jack. The power of Pan can still heal the Neverland. And when it does, you'd better watch out!"

"Ha, ha, ha." Li'l Jack clapped his hook against his claw. The metallic pinging echoed his sarcasm. "I dealt with that threat long ago. I did away with Pan's heirs, me fairy godmother, in case yer mind's completely gone."

Belle whirred to the porthole. She hung suspended just long enough to hurl a sentence. "Ah, but Captain, what you don't realize, is that you *missed one*."

Out the porthole she flew, as fast as her old fairy wings would carry her. There was no time to spare. If the Neverland was to be saved, she had to get Peter's only remaining heir *now*.

Even if it was just a girl—just an orphaned girl named Piper Pizzinni.

CHAPTER THREE

Flight Failure

Even for January in Seattle, the fog tonight seemed impossibly dense. Good thing, Pip thought, because she was really going for it tonight. The Neverland or bust. Between her size, her dark clothes and the fog, she would be next to invisible.

Red lights from the open drawbridge pulsed, like heartbeats suspended in the night's damp curtain. A ship's horn sounded, signaling its successful passage. The bridge tooted in response, its open jaws slowly leveling to flat roadway once again.

She'd thought of using this bridge quite a while ago. She just hadn't tried it until now. Pudge's jeering had convinced her to go for it. No glory in being known as the kid who tried to do a Peter Pan if she didn't follow through.

The bridge bells stopped dinging, and the safety arms lifted for traffic to resume its onward push. The breath Pip had been holding came out in a whoosh. No point in putting it off. It wouldn't get any easier, that was for sure. She hiked her army surplus backpack a little higher, feeling the awkward shift of the bulk tied beneath. The suspended red velour case held her mother's swords.

The swords were the only thing Pip had left of her parents and their life in the theater. She thought of them as her legacy. Five years ago, Piper had been the most accomplished six-year-old swordsperson in the city. But like anything that made her think too painfully of her missing parents, she tended to avoid the swords. She'd only retrieved them tonight from their hiding place because if she really did make it to the Neverland, if she got the chance to save her parents, she would need these swords.

The first step onto the bridge's sidewalk was the hardest. Her legs felt like over-cooked green beans. But she could do it; she could put one foot in front of the other. It was only another fifty paces to reach the middle.

Reaching the center of the bridge span, Piper hoisted herself onto the broad metal rail, kneeling a moment while she collected the courage to stand. One advantage of pea-soup fog—she couldn't see the water below at all—not with her eyes. Her stomach seemed to see it just fine. Breathing through her nose, she shifted to a squat, and then pushed to her feet.

She wished she could see the sky. She'd wanted

to look at the stars as she aimed for them. Even a seagull in flight would do. Well, she would just have to imagine them. Pip closed her eyes, and stretched her arms out to the sides. She pictured stars and birds. She saw her parents' faces in her mind's eye. Their smiles helped unwind the ropy knot in her gut. With a nod of decision, she opened her eyes, and allowed her weight to tip forward.

Something big buzzed past her nose. Pip jerked her head back, batting the glowing blur away with one hand. What was that, a weird giant firefly? She'd barely recovered her balance when metal on metal crashed behind her. Before she could turn to see what it was, an arm hooked her around the waist, and dragged her off the rail.

"Oh no, you don't!"

She couldn't see the man's face, only a headlight beaming from his bicycle helmet. It lit the screaming-yellow clad arm holding her like a vice. A matching arm appeared, its hand holding the bright face of a cell phone. He dialed 9-1-1.

Piper struggled, trying to get loose. She could run—somewhere—anywhere! But the arm only squeezed tighter.

"Emergency on University Bridge. A kid almost jumped."

She fought harder. The man cursed, yanked her

into the air, and dragged her against his hip. The phone cracked into her head as he tried to keep her still. Sirens wailed. Hot tears flooded down her cheeks.

It wasn't the first time she'd ridden in a fire engine. But it was the first time she'd been too miserable to enjoy it, even a little. The firemen had called CPS. Miss Henning had told them she was a ward of Mrs. Fitch. Now they were driving her back there. Sandwiched between two bulky men in uniforms, all she could do was watch with dread.

Lights flashing, they pulled up to the foster home. The fire truck barely fit on this narrow city street, with cars parked for the night on both sides.

"Come on, little Miss." The lead fireman looked at the house, and back at Piper. His eyes revealed a flash of sympathy. "Let's get this over with, shall we?"

Piper didn't bother to answer. She slid over and allowed the man to help her down onto the sidewalk. Her whole body felt like lead. This was the very worst thing she could have imagined. No flight to the Neverland, and no quick end, either. The pain she was in for wouldn't be nearly as brief.

CHAPTER FOUR

Fetching Pan's Heir

Belle ignored her fatigue as she flew. Li'l Jack and Sincoraz would be out tonight hunting the same game as she. Belle had to get there first. Fortunately, the more distance she put between her and the Neverland's ravaged shores, the more energy she had. She didn't allow her mind to travel the road of what would happen to her if the Neverland drew its last breath.

Dropping through a layer of clouds, she saw Seattle's world-renowned landmark looming below her: the Space Needle. This was the neighborhood where Piper and her parents used to live. From here she angled northeast, following the sirens shrieking toward Pill Hill. Now, slightly to the west, until she spotted a shabby, gray, flat-roofed building squeezed between grand old Victorian style houses. She sped toward a lit second-story window and peered inside.

A frumpy middle-aged woman sat at her dressing table, squinting in the mirror as she rolled ugly poky-looking curlers into her hair. Wrong window. This must be the foster mother's room. Belle fluffed her own short strawberry-blonde hair, grateful she didn't have to go through any such torture to make herself beautiful. Not that she didn't have her own beauty tricks.

She zoomed over the roof and dropped to a dimmer window on the other side. Landing on the corner of the windowsill, she peeked in. A whole gaggle of girls—this must be the place. But her Pan-sensor didn't pulse.

Belle flew around the house to a narrow, high window angled open a crack. Ah. Definite Pan-sensor activity here. She squeezed in. Heaving herself up to perch on top of a light fixture, she cursed with the effort. This was why she didn't let anyone call her "Tink." It wasn't seemly for an aging—make that middle-aged—fairy.

Belle eyed the child on the bathroom floor below. Sitting cross-legged, the girl clutched her belly with one arm while half-heartedly scrubbing the tile floor with a toothbrush. Tears coursed down the girl's cheeks. She was silent, but her shoulders shuddered with repressed sobs.

The kid was pitiful-looking. She wore blue jeans, worn and patched at the knees. Her too-big sweatshirt belonged in a ragbag instead of on the girl's skinny upper frame. Holes crowned her too-small high-topped tennis shoes, allowing white-socked big toes to pop out and breathe. A swollen black-and-blue eye and a grim expression completed the picture.

She didn't look anything like Peter. Belle felt relieved. The girl's hair, while short, was dark, not reddish-brown. Poking out in all directions, it was even scruffier than Peter's had been. Belle leaned the other way, cantilevering herself over the light fixture to see the girl's other eye.

When she saw it, she froze. The round green eye, rimmed in wet, dark lashes, could have been Peter's own. Belle had only seen Peter cry once. She shuddered at the memory. It had been over that ratty girl, Wendy. But looking at the green eye below, dripping tears onto the girl's olive-toned cheeks, Belle's heart hollowed with pain. She didn't need her Pan-sensor. She knew, just from the pain in her heart, that this was Peter Pan's granddaughter.

Belle felt as if the air had been squeezed out of her. This was it. Time to face her doom. She'd found Peter's heir, and the girl was a sniveling, useless mess.

🗡

Pip gripped her stomach, hoping the pressure would suffocate her sobs. She'd tried to keep from crying. She'd taken Fitch's blows without a sound.

She hadn't so much as twitched when the old bag tore off her backpack, red velour sword sheath still attached, and locked it in the cupboard under the stairs. She'd almost managed to keep her face a careful blank while being dragged up the stairs by her ear and marched past the girls' dorm room. She'd known without looking that they were all staring, trying to catch a glimpse of the newest girl getting what was coming to her. She knew they wanted nothing more than to hear her cry out, to prove they were right about her. She hadn't given them the satisfaction.

Fitch had thrown her to the tile floor in the institutional bathroom, shoved a worn-out toothbrush into one hand, a can of Comet cleanser and a rag into the other. "You aren't coming out until I say it's clean enough," the foster mother crowed. "Let's see if you still have the energy to run away after you've cleaned all the toilets, all the sinks, and the whole floor." She'd slammed the door, but stuck her ugly face back in for a parting shot. "I bet your parents were as good-for-nothing as you are. Their drug lord probably killed them when they didn't pay up."

The shock of the insult slid past her defenses, and Pip felt the blood drain from her face. Fitch smirked with pleasure and slammed the door again.

The sound of the skeleton key locking the bathroom door echoed in the bare room. The metallic ping and click seemed very loud, and very final.

Piper finally let her world crumple, safe as she was from observers. Tears coursed hot on her cheeks, and her gut twisted with pain. But these were nothing compared to the cloud of hopelessness ballooning over her. It felt like a dark shape, pressing down, squeezing out anything good, leaving only black despair in its wake.

Yes, she'd been pulled off of high places many times. Each time, she'd positioned herself to fly off to the Neverland, but she'd always held back. Before tonight, that is.

It hadn't been only Pudge's challenge that sent her to the University Bridge's rail tonight. Today was the fifth anniversary of her parents' disappearance. Today was her eleventh birthday. Her mother had always told her that the number eleven was magic. She'd waited to really try to fly until tonight, believing that the magic of eleven would carry her skyward, like pixie dust.

So tonight she'd really tried. The hopelessness that enveloped her was not because the bug and the cyclist had kept her from flight. She'd known—in that long moment when her body tipped toward the water below—that when her feet left the metal rail, she would go nowhere but down. The glowing bug and the cyclist had saved her life. The trouble was, she couldn't imagine anything worth saving it for. Not now that she knew she could never, ever, fly to the Neverland. She could never save her parents. She would never see them again. A new flood of tears slicked her cheeks, and she worked desperately to swallow her sobs.

Her mind flicked back to that long moment of shifting balance, of leaning over her toes, and beginning to let go. But this time, her mind tracked the edges of her vision.

She saw the glowing orb, in slow motion, journey toward her face. The shroud of fog both softened and intensified its light. She felt wings first brush her cheek, then vibrate past her nose. Instead of the focus she'd actually had at the time, of the parents she wanted to reach, the vision of memory brought her a clear image of the bright flying being. It seemed to be a tiny man wearing a dark tailored suit. He had brown hair, a sweet smile, and translucent wings the same golden color as the crown on his head.

Pip gulped, tears colliding with surprise in a hiccup. Eyes wide open but unseeing, she replayed the memory again. This time, she added sound. There was the low thrum of cars on the bridge behind her, growing louder, then softer, as each one crossed the bridge's metal grating. She could hear the higher noise of the approaching bicycle, tires humming on pavement. And there was something else. It was a voice. Soft, low, and calm—as if spoken inside her head. "Not yet," it said. "Not yet."

She hiccupped again, hysteria winning over sorrow for the moment. Terrific. She was seeing things now. *Mental delusions.* She remembered the term from counseling sessions after her parents disappeared, when she'd overheard therapists conferring. Mental delusions, indeed. It was probably just her survival instinct making an imaginative showing to keep her from offing herself here and now.

She gripped the toothbrush tighter in her hand and set to scrubbing the floor with more will power. It was funny, really. Her parents had raised her surrounded by the magical world of the theater. Illusions made real. Costumes, lights, two-dimensional set pieces, exaggerated make-up and voices projected to be heard in the back row. Love, joy, hatred, anger, confusion, yearning, all these and more had swirled around the seats where Piper sat watching rehearsals, watching performances. Such deep and magical journeys, every one an illusion.

Even the fighting was an illusion. She knew the mechanics of swordplay, the sweat, the fatigue, and yet—a killing blow was never real on stage. So of course, it made sense that in her time of greatest heartbreak, an illusion would appear to try to save her.

Seeing movement out of the corner of her eye, Piper looked up, and began to laugh. This time it wasn't a well-dressed fairy king. This fairy was a slightly disheveled old woman. She had strawberry blonde pixie hair, and she wore a short, blue, filmy dress finished off with leggings and boots. But what really took the cake was her face. High cheekbones and cat-like sparkling blue eyes held an echo of what had once been stunning beauty. Now, she was—well, she was ancient! She must be a hundred years old! She was a tiny great-grandmother fairy trying to look like she was still hip.

Piper laughed until new tears came. It really was terribly funny. If nothing else, her mind had a heck of a sense of humor. She shook her head, and bent to reapply herself to cleaning the floor.

"And just what is so funny, may I ask?" The vision flushed, and crossed her arms defensively. Hovering mid-air, the ancient fairy's wings thrummed like a hummingbird's. As gracefully and precisely as a ballerina, she settled onto the lip of a sink.

Piper choked, and coughed. She wiped her eyes, and wiped them again. She shook her head and blinked, hard, trying to make the apparition disappear. It wouldn't. The great-grandmother fairy was still there. Cautious, Pip reached out her hand to touch it. When her finger brushed the soft blue cloth of the dress, the fairy jerked back.

"Paws off, kid!"

Pip froze, blinking. "You're real?" Her voice croaked, throat still tight from emotion. "Who are you? Am I seeing things?"

"Of course I'm real," the vision said. "I'm Belle, and you're coming with me to the Neverland."

Piper just stared. The words seemed to take forever to enter her brain. When they did, they swirled around, faster and faster, like a dancing dervish. *The Neverland. You're coming with me to the Neverland.*

"Are you ... really a fairy?" Pip asked. Hope and doubt wrestled inside her.

"The Neverland's one and only. Formerly known as Tinker Bell."

"But ... you're too old to be Tinker Bell!"

The fairy snorted. "Long story. No time to tell you now. We've got to go."

The fairy was real! She had come, for *her*, from the Neverland. She would take her to her parents, and they'd all live happily ever after. Magic existed after all, just as she'd been brought up to believe. Relief poured through her limbs. She *hadn't* dreamed that night when her parents were taken. It had been real. The pirate, the ship, the dragon—all real. But why, oh why, had it taken this fairy five years to come for her?

Joy took a jump and a twist, and suddenly Piper was steaming mad. "It's about time," she growled. "What the heck took you so long? You could've come ages ago!"

The fairy flinched, then flashed back. "You think you're all I've had to think about? I'm here now, so now is when we go." The old fairy's color was still high. "Unless you don't have it in you, in which case, I'll be on my way." She flounced into the air and sped toward the high, open window.

"Wait!" Pip cried. Panic gripped like a fist. She was so close. So close! And now she'd gone and said the wrong thing. She was going to miss this once-in-a-lifetime chance completely. She swallowed, throat gone dry. "Please." Her voice came out in a rasp.

The fairy turned, one hand on top of the inward-tilting window. She stared at Pip. She looked angry, and suspicious.

"I'm sorry," Pip hurried on. "I don't know anything about it, you're right. I just ... I really want to go. Please take me with you."

The fairy nodded once. She hummed back to her sink perch, radiating dislike.

Piper stared, hardly daring to breathe. "I can come?"

Great-grandmother Tinker Bell, if that's who she was, shrugged. "How fast can you be ready?"

Pip let out the breath she'd been holding. "Can the other girls come?" She didn't know why she'd asked that. It wasn't like they were her friends.

"No," the fairy snapped. "And you can't tell them where you're going." She seemed flustered. She smoothed her little dress, then her hair. "It's against the rules," she said, lifting her chin.

"They wouldn't believe me anyway." Pip levered herself to her feet, not caring when she upended the can of Comet. "I have to leave them a message, though. It wouldn't be right if I didn't."

Old Tink raised an eyebrow and stared, imperious.

Pip stood on tiptoe, reached into the medicine cabinet and extracted a tube of lipstick. Opening it, she smiled at its bright red color. Perfect. She wrote on the mirror, *I'll be back.*

The fairy looked at the lipstick message and made a derogatory noise. "Hmph." She switched her attention to Piper. "Can you sneak downstairs?"

Piper looked at the winged-old lady like she was crazy. "Do dogs like bones?" There was a nail file in the medicine cabinet—she could pick the bathroom lock easily. There were hairpins, too, for the lock on the cabinet under the stairs. She'd heard Fitch slam the door to the girls' room shut, so sneaking past them wouldn't be hard.

"Okay, smarty pants," the fairy said. She narrowed her eyes and launched herself back toward the open window. Straddling the window's edge, she turned. "Meet me outside the front door," she said, and wriggled through.

Belle perched on the outside lip of the foster home's front doorframe and waited. She clicked her nails, barely containing her anxiety. Seconds, minutes—it felt like hours. Hope tugged. The child had shown some spirit at the end there. Perhaps there was a chance for the Neverland! But it was too soon to know. Right now, she just had to get this girl out of the house and into the air, before it was too late. And it wasn't the foster mother she was worried about.

Unable to resist, she zoomed above the rooftops, looking toward the Space Needle. Peter's daughter and her husband had lived with Piper only a few blocks from there. That was where Captain Li'l Jack and Sincoraz had come for them five years ago. Since he didn't have a Pan-sensor like she did, that was where they would start looking for the heir he had missed.

Sure enough, even through the haze of fog, she saw the glow of fire, and heard wailing sirens speeding toward what had to be damage done by the black dragon. Her heart froze, then beat far too fast. He might not have a Pan-sensor, but Li'l Jack had a sixth sense when it came to her. It wouldn't take him very long to find her here, and with her, Peter's heir.

Just when she turned to find a way inside to look for the child, the door burst open.

Piper ran out, muddy-green canvas backpack slung over her shoulders, a long red velour package tied to the bottom. "Come on, fairy, whoever you are," she cried as she dashed away from the house. "Fitch is coming, you'd better be quick!"

Summoning all her power, Belle peppered fairy dust over the girl. It was all she had, so it better be enough. Renewing her supply would take a few days. When you were a couple hundred years old, things just didn't work like they used to.

Belle dove to the girl's eye level. "Think lovely, wonderful thoughts!" she commanded.

The girl stopped in her tracks and concentrated. The furrow in her brow deepened.

"Wonderful thoughts! Not angry thoughts!"

Belle yanked the hood of the girl's sweatshirt to keep her moving.

Frowning, the child tried again. Her eyes moved up as she imagined something. Nothing happened. She met Belle's eyes. Was that it, was she doing it right?

"Stop her!" The bad-hair foster mother hollered from the front steps. Lights blinked on in the adjacent houses. No time to lose. Belle dove again, this time to Piper's waist. The back belt-loop would do. Grabbing hold, she took off, drawing the pixie-dusted child up through the air with her.

The girl's gasp of wonder tickled Belle's fancy. No matter the child was just a girl and it wouldn't take much to amaze her. It still felt good.

Belle steered in the direction that would take them farthest from Sincoraz and Li'l Jack. She didn't think. Hanging by her belt loop, the kid now faced the drama.

"Look, a fire!" Pip called. "It's near the Space Needle. See it? The top is always outlined in lights." Silence as the child took it in. "Hey, I used to live over there!" she cried.

"I know," Belle muttered under her breath. "Believe me, I know." She changed her direction, seeking to distract the girl, as if the child's interest might draw the gaze of Sincoraz, and with it, that of

Captain Li'l Jack. "Come on," Belle said, "help me out here. Try the lovely thoughts again, will you?"

She was a tiny great grandmother fairy trying to look like she was still hip.

CHAPTER FIVE

Unwelcome Discoveries

A nd so it was that Piper found herself sailing through the night sky toward the Neverland, butt-first.

She felt a shiver of pleasure in her tummy. Glee sparkled in her limbs. As it did, her body floated up toward the fairy. She almost flattened out.

"You're doing it!" Belle shouted.

"I am? What am I doing?" Pip thought hard about it. Immediately, she sank back to where she'd been before.

"Well, you *were* doing it. Try again. Think of something that makes you *happy*!"

Piper thought about her parents. She saw the faces she loved in her mind, and sadness filled her.

"No, that's not it!" The fairy snapped.

Pip tried again. She thought about skewering that nasty pirate. The one with hook and claw who'd taken her parents. Anger rushed in, and she returned to her doubled-over position.

"Aw, forget it. We'll work on it later. I'll take it from here."

Discouraged, Pip stopped remembering and just paid attention to the glow of Seattle fading into the distance. The fog, so dense when she'd stood on University Bridge, had thinned, making the city below show clearly in patches. The twinkling lights softened as they flew higher and higher.

Finally the bright moonlight beaming around her eclipsed all the lit places below. Her nose stung as she breathed the cold air. Clouds soft as silk brushed by. She felt tiny in the deep quiet of the vast sky through which they flew.

Between the thrill, the quiet, and her exhaustion from all that had happened today, Piper couldn't keep her eyes open. She welcomed the peace of sleep.

The next thing Pip knew, she'd landed in a tangle on hard ground. Pushing herself to her knees, she shook her head and looked for the fairy.

Belle sprawled on a large rock nearby, next to a huge old tree. She looked all tired out. "We're here, sleepyhead."

"Where?" Pip struggled to her feet. The swords banged her behind as she stood.

"The Neverland." Belle pointed to the enormous dead tree next to her. "This is the Never Tree. It used to be inside Peter's Underground Home. They sawed it off every day in the morning, and used it for a table at dinner." She stopped, remembering, then sighed and shrugged. "Then Peter left, and it grew."

Pip stared around her. This had been a forest once. Now barren trees stood, skeletons against a gray sky. Broken-off, hollow trunks encircled her. Charred ground reached in every direction. Boulders, like the one Belle sat on, lay strewn like a giant's game of marbles. The only colors she saw were shades of brown, black, and gray.

The circle of broken-off hollow trees around her brought a dim flash of memory. She counted them—there were seven. Could it be they were the entrances to the Underground Home where the Lost Boys and Peter had lived? No. She dismissed the thought. It couldn't be.

"This can't be the Neverland." Pip croaked. "You're joking, right?" It looked like a place zombies might rise up out of, a place with an evil spell on it.

"I wish I were." Belle leaned back on her hands. She stretched her feet out in front of her as she stared at their grim surroundings. "All this is Sincoraz's doing."

"Who's Sincoraz?" Pip asked.

"It's a dragon. It feeds off life force. Most any life force. That's what it needs to thrive. At first, when Sincoraz arrived, everything stayed more or less in balance, but then—" Belle hesitated. "Well, soon it consumed almost everything living. We fairies started aging. Most died. In fact, I'm the last fairy here in the Neverland."

"I'm sorry," Pip said. Belle looked so sad. She didn't know what else to say.

Suddenly, the fairy's words sunk in.

"So where is it?" Piper looked up, then all around, expecting the humongous black winged lizard she'd seen five years ago (carrying the *Jolly Roger* away with her parents in it) to swoop down and burn her to a crisp.

"Sincoraz lives in the heart of the Neverland, deep in a pit of its own making." Belle shrugged. "I'll show you eventually."

Pip's mind whirled. What did this mean? The Neverland: dead looking and empty. "What about the pirates? Did the dragon kill all the pirates?" Would her parents' captor still be alive?

"Oh no." Belle gave a sharp laugh. "Captain Li'l Jack has an *understanding* with Sincoraz. It doesn't eat pirates." She looked pointedly at Pip. "Fortunately for you, it doesn't eat children either. Says they aren't ripe yet." She made a derisive noise. "But frankly, I have my doubts. I'd steer clear of it, if I were you."

The old fairy's gaze swept the area around them. "And fortunately for me, there are other things it doesn't like, too. Mostly insects. Also toadstools, snakes, worms and spiders. So I've had a little company." Her eyes again settled on Pip. "But you're here now. I brought you to change all that."

"What are you talking about?" Pip stared at the wind-blown fairy. "I can't kill a dragon. Not even with my swords."

Belle laughed, this time a brighter, happier sound. "Oh, no. You'll fix it all because you are Peter's heir. Nothing is as powerful as the joy-filled heart of Pan."

Pip blinked twice and poked her fingers in her ears to see if something blocked her hearing. "I'm who?"

"Peter Pan's heir. His granddaughter, in fact."

"I am?" Feelings of all colors shot through Pip. Voices spoke on top of each other in her head.

Yesss! I knew it!

Like heck you are. If you are Pan's heir, you could've come here long ago.

Pan doesn't need parents. If you're his heir, you wouldn't care so much about saving yours.

That's a load of crap. This fairy is old and crazy.

You were right. That's why the pirate came for your parents. It really is your fault he stole them away.

Pip shook her head to quiet the noise. "Who are you, anyway?" she blurted.

"Like I told you, I'm Belle. Used to be called

Tinker Bell. I was Peter's very-own fairy. Until he left, that is." She grimaced.

"Like I said, you're too old to be Tinker Bell."

The pixie shrugged. "Time started to pass after Peter left. Slowly at first, then faster and faster. The few Lost Boys still here started to grow up. Most left, a few joined the pirates." Belle made a face. "I actually look pretty darn good, considering." She fluffed her hair and smoothed her dress. "I changed my name to suit my more mature self."

Pip backed away. "I don't care about your problems or what you want me to do here. I came here for a reason of my own: to save my parents from that pirate. That—Captain Li'l Jack, right?"

"You came here ... " Belle trailed off. Her face grew pale. "What do you mean, you came to save your parents?"

"That pirate took my parents five years ago. He left in the *Jolly Roger*, carried by the dragon—Sincoraz. My parents were onboard."

Belle looked even paler. "You know about that?" She sat cross-legged, elbows on knees, chin propped in the heels of her hands. For the first time, she looked troubled.

"Yes," Pip said. She spoke firmly to drown out the quivers of fear whispering through her. "I came to the Neverland to rescue them. That's why I brought my mother's swords with me."

"Your mother's swords." Belle raised an eyebrow, color coming back into her face. "She was a swordswoman?"

"The best. She taught me when I was tiny, and I haven't forgotten how. My mother could fight, dance, laugh, sing—she was, *is*," Pip corrected herself, "The best mother ever."

"Of course she could do all those things." In the same cross-legged seated position, Belle now floated a foot above the boulder. She seemed to be losing patience, and with it, gravity's influence. "Your mother was Peter Pan's daughter. But those swords weren't hers. They were Peter's. She got them from him."

"No." Pip shook her head, hating the twist of rising panic.

"Yes." Belle sank back to the rock and glared at Pip. Hands on hips, fire in her eyes, she looked like a fairy berserker. "You don't look anything like Peter, you know."

"I look like my father," Pip retorted.

"Ah yes, your father." Belle's tone dripped with sarcasm.

"My father was the most talented set designer in

Seattle." Pip wouldn't stand here and listen to this old fairy's insults.

"Set designer, you say. Ha! What good is that? I need heart and laughter, and a joy-filled youth like Peter! Instead, I get your scowling face." Belle flew over Pip's head in uneven circles, spewing disappointment. "Peter's granddaughter. The daughter of some man who drew pictures. If Peter's heir had to be a girl, it should've been your mother, not you. At least *she* knew how to think lovely, wonderful thoughts!"

"Well, why didn't you bring *her* here instead?" Pip yelled back.

"She was too old by the time I needed help. When she was young, I had things handled!"

Pip batted the air over her head to keep Belle at bay. "You did, huh? Yeah, it really looks like you've got things handled." She hollered the sarcastic words, gesturing at the barren landscape around them.

"You're hardly in a position to criticize." Belle's wings fairly buzzed as she flew at Piper. Her grimace added even more wrinkles to her fairy face. "You've spent the last five years bouncing from one foster home to another."

"Well, so what if I did? Whose fault is that? And who needs you, anyway?" Pip felt her throat squeeze with tears. "I'm going to find the pirates and get my parents back."

"How're you going to get there? Fly?" Belle taunted.

"No." Pip bit her trembling lip. "I'm going to walk on my own two feet. Just tell me where the *Jolly Roger* is anchored."

Belle hovered, arms folded over her chest. She buzzed there, saying nothing for several moments. Finally she stuck out an arm and pointed. "Take twenty steps that way, and you'll see a trickle of water. The trickle grows to Kidd's Creek, which dumps into Kidd's Cove. That's where the *Jolly Roger* is moored."

Pip nodded, and walked off in search of her parents.

CHAPTER SIX

The Wyrm's Welcome

Pip hadn't walked more than an hour when she glimpsed the distant dull gleam of dim light on dark water. The sea. While the creek continued to wind to her left, she thought if she cut to the right, she'd reach the cove sooner. A shortcut.

Feeling pleased, she angled in the chosen direction. The underbrush grew thicker. Dead-looking, thorny brambles slowed her progress and forced her farther to the right. She tried to cut through, but her ankles and shins began to bleed, scratched even through jeans. More than once she stopped to pull thorns out of the soles of her old high top tennis shoes.

"Darn it," Pip sighed in frustration. The only thing she could do was keep following the clear spaces. She thought of the foster girls back at Fitch's—the Lifers. If only they were here to help her and keep her company! Then again, she'd probably just let them down, too.

Soon the pitch changed and she was climbing. It was a hill. A very big hill. Every time she thought she'd reached the top, it turned out to be only the beginning of another rise. Up the steep sloping terrain she struggled.

She'd completely lost sight of the cove. The foothills had grown larger than foothills. She was lost in the mountains, and from her patchwork glimpses of the sky, not much daylight remained.

Suddenly, she heard, or felt, a sort of rumble. She stopped in her tracks and waited, wondering if it was an earthquake, or a thunderstorm about to drop its cold wet load on her aching body. She heard it again. No, it wasn't either of those things. It was something—over in *that* direction.

Pip half-crouched as she crept up the slope. The rumbling grew louder. The crest of the hill lay just ahead. She chose one of the boulders perched at the top, dropped to her belly, and pulled herself toward it. Digging her fingers into the dirt, slowly, carefully, she lifted her head until she could see over the edge.

The sight that met her eyes tore through her like a scream, and her blood seemed to freeze in her veins.

A large crater spread below. It looked like the Neverland had been struck by a meteor. To her right lay the opening to the dragon's lair. She knew because the dragon itself, Sincoraz, slowly slithered out of the cave's entrance. Black, scaled wings folded against its wormlike body. It reeked of sulfur. The rumble came from its footfalls. This creature would strike terror into the heart of any human.

But that wasn't all. On the other side of the crater from where Pip lay hidden, a path zigzagged its way from top to bottom. The path wasn't empty. Pirates marched a group of prisoners into the crater. The captives, all men, wore orange jumpsuits, and handcuffs. If the movies she'd seen were right, they were straight out of jail. The men looked shell-shocked. Their faces shone, skin sweat-slicked.

The pirates flanking them were armed with swords and pistols. Step by step, they forced the terrified group down the path. When the first group reached the crater bottom, they turned and shouted, trying to make their way back up. Blows rained down, and the group advanced, though the shouting continued. In moments, the group stood only fifty paces from the black beast.

"Avast, ye mealy-mouthed bilge bags! Stop yer confounded caterwauling!"

The voice jolted Pip's heart into double-time. It was *that* pirate. The one who haunted her dreams. The one who'd taken her parents. Captain Li'l Jack. He stood between the prisoners and the dragon. As if to confirm her assumption, he spoke again.

"I am Captain Li'l Jack. It has been me pleasure to chart the course of yer journey up 'til now. At this point, however, we part ways. I bid ye me fond farewell." He bowed low, a mocking grin on his face. Snapping upright, he turned to the terrible black winged lizard. "Are ye ready?"

A cloud of steam shot from its snout and its glowing red eyes began to whirl in response. Pip thought she heard a hissing "yesssss."

"All right, men. On three!" Captain Li'l Jack directed his crew. "One, two, th——" Before he'd finished "Three," the Captain and his men ran, diving for the far sides of the crater.

The giant wyrm opened its maw and inhaled. Before her very eyes, Pip watched the bodies of the prisoners, men from *her* world, disintegrate—like an image fading on a computer screen. There one moment, gone the next. Almost as if they'd been "beamed" to another location, like on the old Star Trek re-runs she'd seen on TV.

Pip peered around frantically, hoping to see the group reappear on the crater's opposite rim. They might be criminals, but surely they didn't deserve to be inhaled by a dragon. But no. All she saw was the dragon backing toward its lair, one rumbling footfall at a time.

"Back to the ship, men!" the Captain ordered.

"Aye aye, Cap'n," the pirates hollered as they scrambled up the steep slope and faded into the underbrush. They obviously couldn't wait to put some distance between themselves and the man-eating lizard.

Captain Li'l Jack, however, drew closer to the terrible beast. "Time for the offering, me pretty." He crooned a pirate tune as he untied a length of rope from his waist, and flung one end over the beast's neck. Holding both ends tight, he leaned back and climbed the rope, hook over claw. His feet walked up first Sincoraz' foreleg, then its chest, until he stood at eye level with it. Reaching into his cloak, he withdrew a silver vial. Uncorking it, the pirate balanced, waiting.

From each dragon eye, now whirling gold instead of red, rolled a very large dragon tear. Captain Li'l Jack moved swiftly, collecting the tears in his vial. Once finished he climbed down, resettled the corked vial inside his cloak, and bowed low.

"Until ye feed again." He rose and strode in the direction his crew had gone, disappearing over the crater's rim.

Piper watched him go. Suddenly it was as if she saw her parents standing in the crater where the prisoners had been moments before. Her father in his black pajamas, dark stubble on his chin. Her mother in her white nightgown, her beautiful hair cascading over her shoulders. Then they, too, disintegrated, as the other prisoners had. Gone. Gone forever.

Blackness pressed at the edges of Piper's sight, and her fingers, clutching the earth, let go. She slid down the bank the way she'd come, rolling into brambles and darkness.

CHAPTER SEVEN

Small Comforts

Piper woke to sunshine, the dusty-looking orb already high in the sky. She rubbed her swollen eyes and tried to orient herself.

"Easy, don't move too fast. Drink this first." Belle handed her a toadstool's cap, filled with clear liquid.

Propping herself up on one elbow, she accepted the offering and sipped. It tasted sweet. "What is this? Where would anything sweet come from in this horrid place?"

The fairy looked miffed. "It's not horrid. It's just dying."

Pip glared at the pint-sized great-grandmother with wings. No—she didn't look anything like a grandmother. Too fancy. She looked worldly, and—well—like an aging Tinker Bell. "You know, you're the last person I want to see today."

"I'm not a person. I'm a fairy."

"Why do you call yourself 'Bell,' anyway? Like ding-dong crazy?"

"No. Belle with an *e*. Like belle of the ball. It's

French for 'beautiful.'" Belle fluttered up to perch on a branch at Pip's eye level and batted her eyelashes.

Branch? Pip took note of where she was for the first time. Shouldn't she be in a tangle of thorny brambles? Instead she lay in a hammock lined with birch bark. Delicate strands of spider web stretched from both ends of the hammock to the large tree branch above her. About ten feet of space stretched between her and the ground. Recognition sparked. This was Peter's Never Tree.

The tree had been grand in its day. Limbs gnarled, arms spread wide, it was a perfect climbing tree. But it sported not a single leaf or acorn. It looked dead, or at least fast asleep.

"How did I get here? Who made the hammock?" Pip gulped the rest of the liquid from her toadstool cup and sat up. "And what is this stuff? It's sweet, and I'm already full."

"Slow down. One question at a time." Belle reached for Pip's cup and inverted it on her branch, settling herself beside it on the rough bark as if it were the world's most luxurious chair. "My friends, the spiders, helped me make your hammock. They spun the web. I collected the bark." She pointed.

Pip followed her gesture to the scattered fallen trees below. Sure enough, there was plenty of bark to collect without stripping it from those still standing.

She patted the tree that now served as her shelter. "It reminds me of my bedroom at home." The mural her father had painted on one wall shone in her mind's eye. Sadness squeezed her throat. Belle looked uncomfortable. "In answer to your other questions, that was spring water with honey in it. Sincoraz doesn't like bees. And I brought you here." She stared at the hammock, as if unwilling to meet Piper's eyes.

"I flew to Kidd's Cove. When I didn't find you, and Captain Li'l Jack and his crew weren't aboard the *Jolly Roger*, I had a terrible feeling where you might be. Unfortunately, I was right." Belle brushed her dress off briskly as if she could brush off the horror of what Piper had seen just as easily.

Pip stared at Belle. She felt numb. When the fairy met her eyes, Pip read aloof defensiveness on her face. So the pixie felt responsible, somehow. Pip let the ragged dread inside breathe, just a tiny bit. "That's what happened to them, isn't it? My parents. Captain Li'l Jack took them to Sincoraz."

The hard lines of Belle's expression melted and her eyes filled with tears. "I'm *so* sorry." She sat blinking rapidly, and then a queer laugh bubbled up. "I can't waste these." She flew to Piper's ankles. "Roll up your pants. Fairy tears heal wounds on contact."

She tended Pip's scrapes and scratches, sprinkling bits of tears here and there.

Pip inspected Belle's work. "Wow. They're all gone." She stared at Belle, an unspoken question in her eyes.

"What?"

"You don't have other magical abilities, do you?"

"Like what? I can do all kinds of things." Belle seemed to swell slightly.

"I mean—you can't—bring people back to life, can you?" Pip saw Belle's bleak look and hurried on. "I know you came back to life after you drank Peter's medicine. I've seen the play *Peter Pan* about a million times," she explained.

"There's a play about us?" Belle's eyes grew round.

"Sure," Pip said. "Books, too, and movies. Anyway, Hook poisoned Peter's medicine, and you drank it to save Peter. You were dying. Peter asks children everywhere to clap their hands if they believe in fairies. Everyone claps, of course, and you come back to life. There isn't something like that for ... people?" Pip trailed off.

"You mean, can I snap my fingers and say 'I believe in Peter Pan?'" Belle's wings sagged. She looked forlorn.

"Something like that, I guess." Pip sighed. "Peter Pan, or Angela Baker and Giorgio Pizzinni."

Belle flew to Pip's shoulder and spoke quietly in her ear. "Those were their names, right? Your parents' names."

Pip felt her hair being stroked by tiny fingers. It sort of tickled. If she hadn't felt so sad, she would have giggled. She took a deep breath instead. "Yes. Those were their names. They've been gone a long time now. Five years. I just didn't know it. Well … maybe I knew," she said softly. "But I didn't want to believe it."

They sat together in silence for a while, a young girl with an old fairy sitting on her shoulder. The hammock swayed gently in a breeze as light as breath. The few remaining dewdrops glistening on the spider webs mirrored the sun, flashing colorful prisms of light.

Pip stirred. "Well."

"Well." Belle rose into the air, suddenly all business. "I thought we'd start the day with a swim for you in Mermaid's Lagoon. There aren't any mermaids left, but there's some old dried soap weed."

Pip glowered. "Are you saying I need a bath?"

The pixie rolled her eyes. "Besides getting clean, it's an excellent place for flying lessons. Our first priority is to get you into the air. Next, you can crow, and then with the help of your trusty swords, we'll see about clearing the villainy out of the Neverland." Belle gestured higher in the tree with her head.

Piper saw that the velour-wrapped swords hung in a tiny hammock of their own. "Okay," she sighed. "Okay to the swim that is, and maybe to the flying lessons. We'll see after that." Under her breath she added, "I need to come up with a plan."

She stepped from the hammock to a broad limb. Balancing carefully, she reached up and unhooked her backpack from its peg of a broken branch before climbing from there to the ground.

"Uh … thanks, Belle," Pip mumbled without looking at her. "Thanks for all this." She gestured to the tree. "You found a place for everything. The camp is magical. Plus you fed me and healed my wounds."

"You're welcome," Belle trilled.

"But," she gave Belle a sharp look, "you still have a lot to answer for, as far as I'm concerned."

The fairy seemed very busy examining the tree bark.

"If you knew that pirate captured my parents," Pip hurried on, "why didn't you come for me sooner?" Her voice cracked with longing. Embarrassed, she growled, "If you'd come right away, maybe they could've been saved."

Belle answered stiffly, not looking at her. "There wouldn't have been anything you could have done."

Pip thought of the scene she'd witnessed the night before and shuddered. If the pirate had taken her parents straight to Sincoraz, the fairy was right.

An awful thought occurred to her. "Maybe Sincoraz didn't even bother to unwind himself from the *Jolly Roger* before killing them. Maybe he just turned his head and inhaled while they were still outside our apartment in Seattle."

"No," Belle snapped, with a shake of her head. "It's a ritual," she explained, her tone gentling. "The dragon eats when Captain Li'l Jack brings food to its lair."

A dark, knotted feeling pressed at Piper's ribcage. "Captain Li'l Jack." The name tasted vile when she said it. She stared in the general direction of Kidd's Cove. Her hand gripped an imaginary sword at her waist. "I can't save my parents," she said, "but I can avenge them. So that's exactly what I'll do."

"I can't save my parents," Piper said, *"but I can avenge them."*

CHAPTER EIGHT

Negotiations

"**D**on't you have *anything* cheerful you can think about?" Belle knew she sounded as exasperated as she felt.

Apparently not. The girl had climbed for the umpteenth time to the top of Marooners' Rock. It was the perfect spot for flying, or for high diving as the case may be. So far it had been all diving with a few body-flops and cannonballs mixed in. The kid must be made of stone. The only direction she flew was down.

The girl summoned an intense look of concentration, inhaled, and leapt out into the air.

Belle knew it wouldn't work before she heard the splash. "Nope," she said, throwing up her hands in frustration. "I've seen furious, determined, longing, and heart-broken on that face."

It didn't matter that only the barnacles heard.

The child surfaced, sputtering and out of earshot.

"But not a single sunny face." Belle frowned and continued. "A few smiles, but not real ones. I need one like Peter's that starts at your toes and ends at your nose."

She flopped into the silky round of a seashell left behind by the mermaids on the rocky ledge where she rested. Playing flight cheerleader for the last hour had exhausted her.

She scowled, caressing the shell's enamel. "Vain she-creatures, those mermaids. They always did think far too much of Peter."

"I can't take any more of this," Pip shouted as she thrashed in the saltwater. "I'm through." Instead of swimming back to Marooners' Rock, she angled toward shore.

"Wait. Wait!" Belle flew to water level, skimming a few inches above the sea and speaking each time the girl turned toward her to breathe. The girl's stroke was steady and strong. She had excellent form.

While the kid was underwater, Belle growled, "Too bad you don't fly as well as you swim." To the child's face she wheedled, "Come on, do you have to be that way about it?" Let's sit on Marooners' Rock together for a bit and talk."

Water spat in her direction.

"Oh, all right!" Belle increased her altitude. "Be that way. I'll wait for you on the beach." She flew ahead in a huff.

"I feel for you, honest," she muttered to herself.

"It couldn't have been any fun stumbling on Li'l Jack feeding that beast. Not to mention realizing your parents were dragon fodder." Belle shivered. "Gave me the willies. I've known him since he was a tyke, but none of his childhood pranks ever came close to this." She found a new enameled seashell and settled in to recover a bit of her spent energy. "Good thing you don't know that poor lot of jailbirds got collected last night while he was looking for you."

Talking aloud to herself made her look crazy, Belle knew, but it was a habit she wasn't about to change. After Peter had left it had been a comfort. These days it actually seemed to help her think.

She watched the child swimming toward her and sighed. "No, it couldn't have been easy for you, kid. But you need to forget about it. Move on. The Neverland needs saving!" If this girl wasn't up to reviving her precious home, Belle didn't know what she'd do.

Finally, the girl reached the shallows and waded to shore. Choosing a dry patch of sand near Belle, she stretched out in the sun. Rivulets ran from her clothes. At least the unfashionable garb had served to protect the child. She'd really smacked the water hard a few times.

Eventually the kid spoke. "It's no good. We'll have to think of another way."

"Another way to fly?" Belle couldn't disguise her disgust. "You think I'm going to drag you around by the belt loop forever?"

"Sure you will," the girl snapped. "If you need me badly enough." She lay in silence for a while, arms crossed, brow knit. "I didn't mean flying. I meant another way to defeat Captain Li'l Jack."

Belle stared at the girl, calculating. That way lay quicksand. She'd known the kid would want to fight the pirate captain, but she had no intention of letting anything truly awful happen to Li'l Jack. She needed to keep this child's attention focused elsewhere.

Actually, she'd hoped Peter's heir could revive the Neverland just by showing up. No fighting necessary. She'd imagined she'd be as full of *joie de vivre* as Peter had been, and things would start to come to life of their own accord. The girl would fly, crow, and laugh, and blooms would burst forth. Time would stop and all would be well. After all, no amount of evil could overcome true joy.

But it wasn't working out that way. So now what? Belle cleared her throat. "What did you have in mind?"

The kid turned toward her. "I was thinking. Peter had a gang. He had back-up."

"You mean the Lost Boys?"

"And you, of course."

"I was never 'back-up.'" Belle knew she sounded peevish. *Hardly a mature response.* She gave herself a mental nudge to mind her manners.

The girl shrugged. "Have it your way. I just meant when he was in trouble, you helped him out."

"Oh." Belle rearranged her wings. Maybe Peter's heir hadn't meant to insult her. "So anyway, kid, you were saying?"

"Kid?" The girl turned to Belle and glared. "Do you even *know* my name? Or do you only know Peter Pan was my grandfather?"

"Of course I know your name," Belle retorted.

"Yeah? What is it?"

"Piper Pizzinni," Belle said primly. She didn't look at the child. Why couldn't she have been named Pan? Hadn't the family the sense to pass on the name? But no, Peter himself had become Peter Baker, once adopted. Not only had no one had the sense to change it back, no one had passed it on: this child's mother had given her daughter the father's last name. No wonder the kid had no idea who she really was.

"Pip," the girl said. "You can call me Pip. Or if you can't manage that, call me Pipsqueak." One corner of her mouth curved in a half-smile. "That's what the girls at the foster home called me."

"How about I just call you 'Trouble'?" Belle challenged.

The kid stared at her for several seconds, then nodded. "Maybe that's best. I don't think we're going to be friends anyway."

"Okay, Trouble, then how do you suggest creating back-up for yourself?"

"I was thinking we could go back to the foster home and rescue the other girls. The Lifers. That's what they call themselves."

Belle sneered. "What kind of name is that? Sounds like a prison gang. You should change it to 'The Lost Girls.'"

Pip shook her head. "Too wimpy-sounding. If you're lost, you need to be found. That's no good." She scratched her head while she thought. "We've got to change the idea that girls only get to come to the Neverland for Spring Cleaning, like Wendy." She brightened. "What about 'Piper Pan and her Merry Band'?"

"Hmmm," Belle said. "As in Robin Hood, you mean."

"Yeah!" The kid looked surprised. "You know about Robin Hood?"

"Of course." *Does she think I was born yesterday?*

"Not a bad name." Belle frowned. "You do know I

can't generate enough fairy dust right away to fly all your friends here. How many are there?"

"Seven plus me." Trouble pulled at her lower lip. Belle winced at the not-so-attractive habit. "It would take at least a cycle of the moon to make enough pixie dust for eight of you, plus there's flying you from here to there first, if you can't do it on your own yet."

Trouble narrowed her eyes. "Very nice of you to remind me."

"You're welcome."

"Hey, I know!" Trouble leapt to her feet.

Sand rained on Belle. "Lippets and starfish! Watch what you're doing, will you?"

"Oh. Sorry." Trouble backed up a step and brushed sand off her pants. "So, do you want to hear my idea, or not?"

"I guess I'm going to hear about it either way." Belle flew to a perch at a safe distance.

"Why not build a ship?"

"A *ship*?" The girl had lost her mind.

"Not a ship, a boat. A small one. So you could cover *it* with pixie dust, and not bother with us kids. Like a sailboat, or—how about a rowboat? A long one." The girl paced as she talked. "I know! We could make a dugout canoe! Maybe the Indians can help us!"

Belle pursed her lips and shook her head. "Long gone. Before Sincoraz got here. The pirates captured all the Indians and made them walk the plank."

Trouble slumped.

Flying in lazy looping circles, Belle considered. Perhaps she could strike a bargain. Something that would not only serve her own ends but would also present no real threat to Li'l Jack. After all, how much mischief could eight girls create? *Girls*, mind you. All sound and no fury. No fun either, if you asked her.

"Tell you what," Belle said. I'll make a deal with you. I'll help get your back-up team, if you promise to learn to fly when we return."

"What if I can't? Fly, that is?" The troublemaker folded her arms and hunched her shoulders in suspicion.

"I don't see how you can possibly be Peter's heir and not be able to fly. You just have to try harder."

Peter's granddaughter narrowed her eyes, regarding her for a long moment. Finally she straightened. "Okay, it's a deal." She spit in her palm and held it out for Belle to shake.

"Ugh. You expect me to touch that?" Belle wrinkled her nose. "I don't think so. You'll have to take my word of honor." Trouble didn't need to know fairies weren't exactly known for sticking to their promises. News for another day.

"A dugout is made from a hollowed-out log, right?" Belle asked. "I think I can find a crew to help you make one." With that, she buzzed into the air, hoisted Trouble by the belt loop, and hauled her back to camp.

†

It would be much more impressive, not to mention dignified, to fly on my own.

When Pip fell in a heap at the foot of her tree, she squawked. "Can't we at least figure out a way to set me down instead of dropping me?"

Belle uttered something unintelligible.

Piper decided to ignore her. She started walking, inspecting the various fallen logs nearby. "This one is just about the right size," she said, pacing it off. "Long enough for three bench seats, wide enough for two abreast, space for one to steer at the rear."

"That's space for seven. What about the eighth?" Belle hovered in the air at Pip's eye level.

"The eighth is Thumb. She's only four. She'll sit in the bow and call the strokes."

Belle nodded. "So you need a small bench front and back, and three wide ones between, right?"

"Yes, and paddles. Six regular paddles, and one a bit larger for steering. A small mast too, if it can be managed. A detachable one."

"To hoist a sail?"

Pip shrugged. "Could be. At least to fly our colors." Her excitement faded. "But how are we going to do all that without any tools?"

"Simple," Belle said. "Delegate."

Ten minutes later, Pip sat on a boulder, watching in awe as Belle gave orders to her crew. The termites were to make the boat, eating away everything except the hull and benches. The carpenter ants set to work on another log making paddles.

"All set," Belle said, looking proud of herself. "You stay here and supervise. There's something I have to take care of." She darted off with a whir of her wings.

"Okay then. Don't hang around and help out or anything," Pip grumbled.

Watching the laboring insects, her eagerness grew. This could really happen! She could go get the other foster girls, and they could all attack the pirates together! Pirates. That reminded her. She needed to make a flag.

Piper searched the ground for a good-sized piece of burned wood. Next, she opened her backpack and pulled out her faded pink baby blanket. Besides her mother's swords, this blanket was her only remembrance of her happy life with her parents. Using the wood as charcoal, she drew skull and crossbones, surrounded by a large circle with a single slash through it. The international sign for "not." First on one side of the blanket, then repeated on the other side.

"Pirates not allowed." Pip savored the words, liking the flavor of anticipated revenge. "Those pirates will never know what hit them."

CHAPTER NINE

Captain Li'l Jack

board the *Jolly Roger*, Captain Li'l Jack roared for his First Mate. "Flea! Fffleeea!" Where the devil had he disappeared to?

"Aye aye, Cap'n." A short, wild-haired pirate whose eyes didn't point in the same direction poked his head into the captain's quarters.

"Where have ye been, Flea?" Li'l Jack purred the question, knowing it threatened more than bellowing.

Flea stepped in, shaking in his shoes. "Guttin' fish, Cap'n." He removed his sailor's cap and scratched his head.

"Isn't that part of the sea cook's trade?"

"Aye, Cap'n, but I knows how ye likes me to keep up me skill with me knife." Flea held up a long knife, still slimy with fish entrails.

"Enough!"

The roar meant all was back to normal for the moment. Flea relaxed, then remembering himself, drew himself up in a military salute.

"It's concert time," the captain said. "Roll out the baby grand, and summon the crew. *All* the crew,

Flea. If anyone's caught below while I'm playing, I'll tear out his heart with me hook." Li'l Jack pulled back his lips in a smile, knowing his gold-capped teeth shone.

"All right, Cap'n." Rather than dashing off, Flea appeared to settle in as he sheathed his knife, clasped his hands in front of him and grinned. From heels to head, he resembled a bow, sway-backed at the middle. "We loves concert time, Cap'n, we does. And if I might say so, Cap'n, y' look right handsome today."

Li'l Jack reached for a nearby jewel-encrusted hand mirror and raised it with his claw, giving his face a careful inspection. "Do I look like Hook, Flea?"

"Oh, aye, Cap'n. Shifty and unsavory, just like ol' Cap'n Hook."

Li'l Jack threw him a grimace that turned the little man's face scarlet and sent him into his customary stuttering.

"I m-mean, Cap'n, y' has the look of a g-great captain, like Hook. But yer ever so m-much more comely than the ol' chap was. Where he was dark, ye're f-fair. Y' has the look of a hero, with them blue eyes."

"That I do," murmured Li'l Jack, combing his faint moustache and goatee with his hook. "I've followed in his footsteps. The greatest pirate of all time: Captain Hook, Terror of the Seven Seas." He paused, his mind taking a detour. "Do ye remember when I arrived in the Neverland, Flea?"

"Aye, Cap'n, I do." The First Mate's color had returned to normal. "Shall I tell ye the story, Cap'n?"

"Aye, Flea." Li'l Jack lowered himself into his favorite red velvet armchair, still gazing into the mirror. "Indulge me." Hearing the account of his arrival in the Neverland soothed him. It was one of his favorite rituals.

He was still feeling jangled from Belle's unexpected appearance. Not to mention her unsavory news, and his failure to find this Pan he'd supposedly missed. Having Flea tell him the tale would make him feel better.

"Ye was the cutest li'l tyke, ye was, Cap'n." Flea chuckled, a fond look in his eyes. "Poor li'l soul, all weepy-eyed ye was, and without normal arms. Ye only had the two short stumps where they'd cut off yer 'fins,' as ye told us."

A glare sent Flea hurrying on.

"But mighty capable stumps they was, Cap'n." A smile of pure affection spread across his Mate's round face. "And there never was such a determined li'l lad. I still remembers, I does. When she brought ye, y' told Tink—I mean, Belle ... " he threw the captain a worried glance.

"She was still 'Tink' then, Flea, no matter. Proceed," he commanded.

"'Y' told her you'd no intention whatsoever of becoming one o' them mealy-mouthed brats, the Lost Boys. Nor like that fool of a flying codfish, Peter Pan. So she left ye here with us." Flea shook his head in admiration. "'Y' knew straight off ye wanted t' grow up and be a man like Hook. A powerful man, respected by all, and feared t' boot."

"Aye." Li'l Jack gazed dreamily into the mirror, seeing himself as he had been so long ago. "I took Hook's fine example to heart, Flea. And when he met his doom in the jaws of the croc, I stepped into his shoes. Indeed," he brandished his hook, "This is Hook's very hook."

"So it is, Cap'n, which I keeps sharp and shining, as y' well knows, t' strike terror in the hearts of the crew and yer enemies."

"Aye," Li'l Jack gloated. "Well, Flea. I'm not a tyke any more, am I?"

"Oh, no, Cap'n." Flea's round face looked horrified. "Last we measured, ye was six feet tall, ye was. But we calls ye Li'l Jack anyway, fer the sake of the dear li'l man ye was."

"Indeed, Flea. For *her* sake as well." Captain Li'l

Jack's eyes wandered to a golden birdcage, outfitted with a tiny royal-looking divan. Its door hung open and it held nothing inside except the former throne of his erstwhile companion and partner in crime, Miss Belle.

"If ye don't mind me askin' Cap'n," Flea queried, his voice hesitant. "Where's the lovely fairy gone? She wasn't but a step or two from your side all those years, until the last handful. Ever since that brat Peter Pan left, she's been like a mother to ye, Cap'n, hasn't she?"

"Aye," the captain said, his mind far away. "Better than a mother. Me own cast me off as useless, born without proper arms and hands as I was. No. Belle's been me fairy godmother. She made me every dream come true.

"Save one." His eyes dropped to his hook and claw, now lying quiet in his lap. "But I don't need her able assistance for that dream. I'm taking care of it on me own." He peered toward the porthole, thinking of his forays for dragon fodder.

Last night's had been productive, save the lack of turning up the Pan Belle had said remained at large. He'd a nose for Pan, he'd been sure he could sniff out any relative. But he hadn't caught the scent last night. Not a whiff.

If only Belle would come back to him, he could

turn her around. They'd rid the world of Pan, whose shade had always been the only thing that kept Belle from adoring him utterly. He'd get his hands, and they would conquer the world together. He would perform, she would applaud. He knew her soft spots. He'd always gotten his way with her. After all, he was the apple of her eye.

His First Mate was staring at him. He drove his hook into the arm of the chair and roared "Confound it, what're ye still standing there for, ye herring-gutted swab?"

Flea turned white, straightened up and saluted. "Yes Cap'n. Right away, Cap'n." He nearly stumbled over his own feet in his haste to leave the cabin.

Li'l Jack listened to the slap of running feet overhead and the clunkety-clunk of the baby grand piano being rolled from its storage place—lashed to the main mast—across the wooden decking to the bow of the ship.

He'd gained the instrument as booty when they'd raided the yacht of a wealthy man and his family. That had been a pretty sight, the family treading water and pleading while the piano was hoisted aboard the *Jolly Roger*. He'd taken pity—he'd stayed the order for their execution. After all, living without their piano was punishment enough. He'd allowed them to board their lifeboat before he'd sunk their yacht. Lovely. He could still hear their cries and smell the tang of exploded gunpowder.

Striding over to face his full-length mirror, Li'l Jack smiled, then bowed. "Thunderous applause, I'll have. Thunderous," he gloated. "For the master concert pianist I'll become once I have real hands." Imagining the roar of an adoring crowd, he bowed again.

Flourishing his hook and claw, he made his way up on deck. "For now," he told himself as he strode down the empty corridors, "I'll make me entrance and use the tools at hand." He gave a crooked grin. "Pun intended."

†

Belle visited her real home on the way to see her protégé, the most ruthless, arrogant pirate captain ever to sail the Seven Seas. If that Trouble girl didn't have what was needed to pull the job off, Belle would have to save her home another way. Perhaps if she pulled out all the stops, she could change Li'l Jack's mind.

"Faery's Nook," she sighed as she approached her dream home. It was nestled in the hollow of a mossy bank, overlooking the Mysterious River. A veritable palace, Li'l Jack and his men had built the

Nook for her long ago when he was a slender young man and his voice still cracked from time to time.

Unbeknownst to the pirate captain, it marked a spot where Belle (then "Tink") and Peter had spent many happy hours playing, laughing and dreaming the days away. It had been their secret place, unknown even to the Lost Boys.

That was before Peter left. She hadn't taken any interest in Li'l Jack until then. He'd only been the oddball boy of the many she'd brought to the Neverland. The one who wanted to be a pirate instead of joining Peter's boys.

Of course she'd never told Li'l Jack of the site's significance. She'd only told him of her dreamed-of fairy castle, and he'd had it built for her.

Made from the burnished stump of a myrtle tree, the Nook was all curves and hand-carved wood. Furnished with silks and velvets, its fairy-size down-filled furniture was fit for a queen. Light poured in windows and skylights, and she could zip in and out wherever, whenever, she pleased.

Entering, Belle took the time for a leisurely bath of bubbles. She chose a gorgeous red dress, jewelry, of course, and dabbed a bit of vanilla behind her ears and at her throat.

"No, Peter, I don't feel guilty," she said aloud, talking to her long-gone admirer as she often did.

"I'm doing exactly what fairies do. Getting the most out of everything I possibly can." She made a face in the mirror at her imaginary audience.

"You left, after all. Who I associate with now is my choice. It has been for a long time, and it still is." Dipping a finger into her secret stash of pixie dust, she sprinkled the sparkling magical stuff all over. One could never overdo glamour.

"And I have to tell you," she said, throwing a backward glance at the mirror on her way out. "Your granddaughter is a tremendous disappointment. It's her fault, in fact, that I have to go see Li'l Jack at all." She floated down the stairwell and exited with grace and her best showmanship. As if Peter were indeed watching.

Heading in the direction of Kidd's Cove, she felt the pit that was Sincoraz's lair before she saw it, near the Neverland's highest peak, sunk in the mighty crater the dragon had made on its arrival. She lost altitude, energy dropping like sand in an hourglass. "I'll go the long way 'round," she growled.

Veering to the right, she drew on her reserves to skim over mountains. No green flanked their sides, nor the valleys between.

She shuddered. "Oh, Peter," she sighed, gazing at the barren land below. "If I don't find a way to remedy all this soon, I'll be not only an old fairy, but a dead one."

Hastening forward, she tried to outfly the feeling of desperation swamping her. "I'll not escape to the Crystal City again, thank you very much. Just because the rest of my kind has retired to the Fairy Kingdom doesn't mean I will."

"Anyway," she snorted, I already tried that. Fat lot of good it did me. Put it this way. I'd much rather be the only fairy here than one of the throngs there." In a rare moment of insight, she laughed at herself. "Not that you'll be surprised to hear it." The laughter helped; she gained altitude and felt better.

As she flew, the mountain ridges flattened into hills, the hills into valleys. Love for her home flooded her heart, and she ached for its stripped condition. "The Neverland is *mine*," she said. "I should never have run away and left it." She thought again of the horror she'd felt when she'd returned from the Fairy Kingdom and found her beloved island so near death. "If it can't survive, I might as well die with it."

Belle's keen hearing picked up the familiar tune of "Chopsticks" before the *Jolly Roger* came into view. The tinny tune swelled, repeating itself over and over as Belle lit on the edge of the ship's deserted crow's nest.

The entire crew clustered below, at attention

around the piano on deck. She wanted to laugh at the glazed expressions on the pirates' faces. They knew better than to show their boredom, or wince at missed notes. Many a sailor had met his end that way.

"I've even suggested creative new ways for Li'l Jack to help the poor souls meet their Maker," she muttered, examining her fingernails. She shrugged. "And what of it?" She brushed at her hair, as if to shake off an unspoken accusation.

The tune slowed dramatically and came to a close. The crew beat their hands together and stamped their feet, pretending zeal as they shouted "Bravo!" and "Encore!" On his feet, Captain Li'l Jack bowed again and again.

Belle settled herself, knowing what came next.

The pirate captain sat back down on the piano bench. "Flea," he bellowed.

"Yes Cap'n." Flea stepped up and snapped off a smart salute.

"You may accompany me." Captain Li'l Jack spoke in the exaggerated tones Hook had taught him to indicate good breeding.

Belle smiled with pride. He really was quite something, her pirate captain.

At a nod from Li'l Jack, Flea began thumping out the two-handed rhythm of "Heart and Soul." After a couple of rounds, Li'l Jack chimed in, using his claw to play the simple melody.

"Poor fellow," Belle murmured. "Dreaming of being a concert pianist, yet you can't play anything requiring more than two fingers." She shook her head in sympathy.

"Still," she added grudgingly, "I won't say I can't understand longing for something. I'd give anything for the way things used to be." She remembered the days of standing on a lily pad and staring at her fabulous reflection for hours. She sighed, desire tinged with frustration.

Flea bungled the accompaniment. His face went red, then white. A nearby crewman chuckled.

How fortunate for her protégé, Belle reflected. Thanks to the crewman's *faux pas*, the captain wouldn't have to shoot his First Mate.

Captain Li'l Jack stopped playing and stared the crewman down. Before the poor man could utter an apology, the captain stood and bellowed his command. "Lock the blighter in the brig. We'll keelhaul him tomorrow at first light."

He strode off, hollering as he went. "Back to work, ye bilge rats, or I'll split yer gizzards." His hook gleamed as it menaced and shook.

"Y' heard the captain," Flea took over, relief

apparent. "Aloft with ye, ye swabs, we're casting off. Hoist the anchor!"

Belle didn't wait for more. "That's my cue," she said, rising from her perch. The *Jolly Roger* would take a turn about the cove and prove its seaworthiness to captain and crew before mooring once more. Now that Li'l Jack had his arrangement with Sincoraz, he no longer sailed far from the Neverland's shores.

The far-flung forays on behalf of Sincoraz were another matter altogether. She didn't want to think about those.

Flitting toward the stern, Belle took the back way to the captain's quarters. With any luck, she'd get there first. Happily, the cabin room door stood slightly ajar. She slipped in just as the captain arrived below.

Belle slid into the hanging birdcage expressly outfitted for her, draped herself onto her regally appointed daybed, and awaited his arrival. She was here to get what she wanted, and she would use every feminine wile she still possessed.

She chuckled. "Almost as if I'd never left."

CHAPTER TEN

Plots and More Plots

Belle watched Li'l Jack swagger into his quarters. The door banged shut behind him. "Temper, temper," she chided.

Li'l Jack spun around and stared. "Ah," he crooned, covering his initial surprise. "Me own private fairy decided to return." Strolling over to the porthole, he opened it, letting in the sharp, briny air. Turning back to her, he looked her up and down, appraising. "That's a pretty rig ye're wearing."

"Why, thank you." Belle preened.

"Not at all. Too bad yer face seems to have aged a good deal in the last five years." At her gasp, he gave an ugly grin and plunked himself into his favorite chair.

"Is that any way to talk to your elders? And betters, I might add." She whipped through the air, fury powering her flight before she realized she'd never accomplish her aim that way. The upper hand was hers now. She needed to be careful not to relinquish her position.

She landed on the small table to the right of the

captain. "You look a bit—tired," she said, her tone concerned.

"Ye think so?" He lifted the hand mirror from the table and inspected himself worriedly.

He never changed. Smiling inwardly, Belle strolled to the edge of the table. "Mmmm." She studied him as a master artist studies her creation. "Perhaps you need to sip a drop of that Life Elixir you so carefully harvest from your dragon friend."

He threw the mirror down with such force that it cracked. His claw grabbed at her. "I'll do no such thing," he snarled. "I've almost enough. Do ye know what that means? The Elixir will generate real hands where I've none! I'll not waste it on petty pursuits."

His eyes narrowed with greed; his lip curled in excitement. "And if ye think ye're going to convince me to use it to restore yer own youth, 'tis folly. I know yer tricks."

Belle widened her eyes in feigned surprise. "Of course you do," she crooned, stroking the claw that clutched her. "My dear good boy. No one knows me better." *Other than Peter*, she thought, *and what good can he do me now?* "I didn't come to fight with you. I came because I *missed* you."

Li'l Jack's grip loosened. He stared at her hand as she petted his steel claw. He couldn't feel the caress, of course, but the sight of it seemed to mesmerize him.

Easing onto the claw, Belle walked up the steel forearm to the elbow. She felt the mechanical joint underfoot before stepping onto real flesh. Long ago, when she'd first taken up with him, he'd confided the story of how his parents decided the malformed digits, or "flippers," he'd been born with should be amputated. He was never even allowed see how useful they could be.

Poor boy. He'd been ripe for her nurturing influence. Bringing him to the Neverland had been an act of mercy. Deciding to adopt him had been sheer genius.

Before Peter left for good, it would never have occurred to Belle to go out of her way for anyone. But in the absence of her dear companion, she'd grown so lonely. Of all the youngsters left in her kingdom, Li'l Jack had the most potential. The "oddball" factor that called him to become a pirate was actually his ambition—a quality even Peter Pan hadn't had.

She'd helped him bring it to fruition.

The fact that he'd adored her in the process hadn't hurt any. She needed to be adored as much as Li'l Jack needed to be powerful. "You are my only protégé, after all," Belle crooned. "Even if we did disagree over—that thing." She waved a hand as though the dividing issue five years ago had been insignificant rather than a matter that doomed her life as she knew it. The night he'd fed Angela Baker and Giorgio Pizzinni to Sincoraz had been the beginning of the end. She'd left for the Crystal City that same night.

"Were ye here in time to hear me performance?" Li'l Jack's gruff tone didn't hide his eagerness.

She laughed, nodding and clapping. "It was *wonderful*."

"Wasn't it though?" He grinned, gold crowns flashing. "Just imagine how marvelous me playing will be with real hands."

"Yes, I'm sure." She cleared her throat. "In a way, that's why I'm here. Becoming a concert pianist will require hours of your time, will it not?" She took his nod as confirmation. "How will the ship run itself without your vigilant eye? Surely you don't think Flea is up to the task."

His brow furrowed, he growled. "Why? What is it ye're suggesting?"

"Oh, nothing at all." Standing on his shoulder, she blew in his ear.

"Heh, heh—that tickles. Stop it, Belle!" The pirate captain wriggled like a little boy.

"I was just thinking how hard it will be for

a man of so many talents to focus on just one."
She fluttered her wings against his neck, eliciting
more laughter. "I don't imagine you'll have time to
continue feeding that silly old dragon. Those raids,
those long flights—an artist needs his rest."

"Ah ha-ha-ha!" Giving a final shudder of ticklish
pleasure, Li'l Jack reached his hook up to flick her
off his shoulder. The hook met not fairy, but air.
"So that's what this is about," he seethed, his mood
changing with the speed of a fairy's.

Belle sat in her "cage" and smiled. The bars were
too widely set to keep her in; it was only a game of
theirs. He played the master, she played the prized
treasure.

"Well, don't worry yer pretty red head about that,
Miss Belle. If anyone can do it all, 'tis I. Besides, I've
been training Flea on the raids."

*Thorns and stingers. He isn't going to stop. I should've
known his greed wouldn't allow it. He wouldn't stop after
killing Piper's parents, even when I begged him to. Why would
he stop now?* Belle kept the frustration from her face.
Wait—something he'd said … "But if Flea runs the
raids, won't that make him the new Dragon Keeper?"

Li'l Jack jammed his hook into the small table,
splintering the wood. "Shut up, ye blasted female!"
he roared. Wrenching his hook free, he leaned back
in his chair, taking a moment to control himself.

"Since ye're so smart, perhaps I'll leave the problem up to you." His voice dripped with the false sugar of rancid honey. "If ye can't come up with something, I'll find me a younger, prettier mother."

She started up before recognizing the bait.

"Ah, but come to think of it, ye don't always get yer way, do ye?" His eyes sparkled and he fairly drooled with glee. "I seem to recall ye *summoned* the mighty Sincoraz, the beast ye so desperately want to get rid of now, didn't ye?

"How did you put it? You got me a 'worthy opponent'? Whose opponent is he now, little mother of mine?" He threw his head back in a laugh.

The sound chilled Belle to the bone. She could not control her fury. She flew at him, stopping in mid-air, level with his blue eyes. "We'll see who has things all figured out. Remember Peter's heir can solve my problem in a flash."

His face froze. "Ye did say that just the other day, didn't ye?" His eyes took on a calculating look. "Tell me this, then. If ye've got this Pan to save yer fool self and yer nasty little world, why are ye here with me?

"Those descendants of Peter's ... " he continued, his tone pitched to bait her. "The lass had spirit— an attractive woman—but her mate was a mangy mongoose. Didn't know a gangplank from a galley."

He smoothed his goatee with his claw. "Fortunately, it didn't put off Sincoraz's appetite. The beast consumed them, Pan's heirs or no. And it will do the same to another Pan, trust me."

"Ah, but it won't," Belle flared. "This one's not *ripe* enough for your dragon friend. So you can forget your schemes, Li'l Jack, and start watching your back." She taunted him, enjoying every second. "Because *this* one is already safe with me!" She hadn't meant to tell him, she really hadn't. Not straight out like this. But she just couldn't help herself. The man had grown too big for his britches.

She darted out the open porthole before Li'l Jack could shut his gaping mouth. "He had that coming, and it felt good," she steamed as she careened blindly overland, returning to Trouble's camp. She didn't even try to gain altitude. As long as she was flying, who cared if it wasn't high? Ignoring a twinge of guilt, she gloried in having had the last word.

The closer she got, the sharper the twinges became. As much as she didn't want Li'l Jack to be killed, neither did she want Trouble's demise. When she saw the girl's form at a distance, curved over the logs where she'd left her, Belle halted, momentarily stricken.

"I did the best thing," she sputtered to the Peter she carried in her mind. "I've no cause to worry about

Trouble, Peter. She can take perfectly good care of herself. She already knew of the pirate captain," Belle tried to convince herself. "I just evened the playing ground. Now both parties will be on their guard."

✝

Captain Li'l Jack stood, hoping to settle the roiling, sick feeling in his belly. "Pan's heir, here?" he breathed. "It can't be!" He wiped beads of perspiration from his forehead. "Ah, but I know that fair firefly all too well," he said, shaking his head. "She might not keep her word, but she cannot lie outright to save her own hide.

"Flea!" He only had to bark the name once before the little man appeared.

"She's ship-shape, Cap'n. Never better. 'Tis a fair wind blowin' and she sailed like an angel." Flea carried on, blind to his captain's agitation. "The crew's workin' like a well-oiled machine. If you ask me, sir, takin' 'em t' see the dragon feed keeps 'em on their toes."

"Shut up, Flea!" the captain growled. "I didn't call ye in to report on the *Jolly Roger*." He stood at the porthole, gazing toward land. "It's that fairy, Flea, she's up to something. I want you to take two men and travel to Pan's old hideaway. That underground home place. Don't let your presence be known. Just see if Belle's there, and who, if anyone, is with her. Then report back to me."

Li'l Jack remained at his post long after his mate shoved off. Did his eyes deceive him? "Blast it all," he cursed, pushing the porthole shut. The longer he gazed at the hills, the more he thought perhaps they wore a fuzz of new growth. "If that's green I see," he hissed, "I'll rip someone's head off with me hook."

†

Pip spotted the incoming bright light plowing toward her like an overgrown hummingbird and ran to meet it. "Belle, look!"

"Can't you give a gal a chance to get settled?"

The fairy's irritation didn't squelch Piper's excitement. "Oh. Sure. Sorry. It's just that ... " She halted, staring at the fairy's long red evening gown. "Wow! That's some dress!"

"Thank you."

Was it her imagination, or did Belle throw her a guilty glance? No matter. The little fireplug wouldn't get under her skin. Not tonight. "Well, when you get a minute, come look!" She dashed back over to the work site.

The progress bowled her over. She'd stood here all afternoon watching them, and it still amazed her.

"Those termites are really something! See?"

Belle perched on a limb above. "Of course. I told you delegating was the way to go."

"Yeah, but I had no idea they could work so fast!" She pointed out the progress. "See? They've already formed the tops of all the benches. Now they're working their way down, hollowing it out as they go." She knew she probably sounded over-enthusiastic. "It already looks like a dugout canoe!"

"Sure wish I could've gotten you to summon that kind of feeling for your flying lesson."

Pip glared half-heartedly at Belle.

"Maybe termites are your lovely, wonderful thought." The fairy shifted her attention to the other log, where the carpenter ants worked. "What about the other crew?"

"They've already divided that log into seven pieces: six the same length and the seventh a little longer. They'll make the oars from those." Piper shook her head. "It's hard to believe. I'd have never thought itty bitty insects could do something like that, so well and so fast."

"Watch it with the 'itty bitty,' kid. Just because something's small doesn't mean it isn't mighty." Belle's mouth curved up in spite of her sharp tone.

Good, Pip thought. She wanted Belle to share her excitement about rescuing the other foster girls. No way could she do it without her help. She'd do whatever it took to stay on the old fairy's good side.

Of course she didn't even want to think about whether the girls would want to come with her. Sure, they'd be happy to leave Fitch's Last Ditch Foster Home, but would they trust her enough to come to a place they didn't believe in? Pip rubbed at her eyes, trying to make the worries go away. She stifled a yawn.

"It's getting late." Belle clapped her hands twice. "Time to blow the whistle for the evening." With a whir of wings and a tinkle of bells, she sent the insect crews marching off in their respective directions.

"Will they be back tomorrow?"

"Of course. Now I'll show you where I've stashed the honey for your spring water. Then we'll watch the sunset, as pale as it is these days, and get to bed. Tomorrow afternoon we'll be on our way. You'll need a good night's sleep."

Pip grinned and for half a second felt like she was floating. As soon as she looked at her feet she was back on the ground. She must've imagined it.

An hour later, she snuggled in her Never Tree-suspended hammock, a new birch bark blanket tucked under her chin. Excitement overruled fatigue.

She had a rescue mission to plot. Not to mention a battle to plan for defeating a pirate captain and his crew. And somewhere in there, she had to make a team out of the suspicious, motley group of girls that called themselves "The Lifers."

†

"Ye were right, Cap'n!"

Seated at the piano, the captain barely looked up from his afternoon scales when Flea reported back. Scales, first with his claw, then with his hook. Practice was a private concern, no audience required. "Well, don't keep me waiting, ye crab-brained swab! Spill the bilge, or cut cables and run!" A twist of his hook and he had the bothersome man by the collar. Without even looking.

Flea stood at attention. His stomach growled. "Y-y-yes, Cap'n." He spoke carefully so the hook at his throat wouldn't puncture flesh. "The fairy was at Pan's old hideout. She seemed to be doin' business with a fleet of insects."

"She was doing *what*, Flea?" Captain Li'l Jack purred the question.

"Er, I don't know exactly, Cap'n. It looked like she was watchin' 'em tear up old logs."

"Odds, bobs, hammer and tongs." Hook's favorite

expression always bought him time to think. It made his men uncomfortable. "Sounds suspicious," he said. "But we'll let that go for the moment. Was she alone?"

"No, Cap'n." Flea's head waggled back and forth like a puppy's tail..

"I knew it!" Anticipation of defeating a truly worthy opponent filled Li'l Jack's heart. Or the spot where he thought his heart would be, if he had one. "Who else was there?"

"Just a slip of a girl, Cap'n."

"A girl? Confound it man, don't mock me. Did ye say a girl?"

"A-aye, Cap'n. Short dark hair, about yea tall, round green eyes, kinda cute, really, Cap'n. A girl."

Li'l Jack stared at his mate until the man's mottled face told him he was telling the truth. "A girl, eh? Imagine, Pan's heir, a girl."

"Pan's heir? Ye mean Peter Pan, Cap'n?" Flea made a sign to ward off evil.

"Stop that foolishness." Li'l Jack's face felt like it might split, his grin stretched so wide. He'd never fought the legendary Peter Pan. He'd been too busy swabbing decks and polishing brass as a lad to do more than glimpse Hook's nemesis. Now he'd have a Pan of his own to challenge.

"There's no cause for alarm," he practically

hummed the words. "None at all. 'Tis almost a disappointment, really. A female is no threat. In fact, a female can be tricked into anything."

The captain punctuated his words with music, gliding his claw over the piano keys, top to bottom in an elegant *glissando*. "I repeat: a female can be tricked into *anything*."

CHAPTER ELEVEN

Foiling Fitch

The flight back to Seattle was ever so much better than being hauled butt-first to the Neverland. Laden with pixie dust, the dugout canoe soared through the air, light as a feather. Pip used her paddle as steering rudder when directed, to keep the boat headed in the right direction. It needed only a very light touch. Her pink blanket with its no-skull-and-crossbones symbol fluttered in the breeze atop the small mast.

Belle's steady light beckoned from the bow. The fairy wore a black dress tonight, and perched on the boat's prow rather than flying.

Piper cleared her throat. "Are you sure you aren't going to a concert or something? You look so formal."

Belle looked at her like she was crazy. "No," she said. "It's camouflage."

Coughing to disguise her laugh, Pip thought it would take a lot more than a black dress to camouflage the pixie's bright light. Not that she'd say it to Belle.

Unlike the "camouflaged" firefly, Pip wore the same old sweatshirt and jeans she'd escaped in. She wanted to talk to Belle about making a set of clothes more fitting for her new position: being Piper Pan. But it hadn't been the right time.

Generous as she'd been, the old fairy had more than a bit of a chip on her shoulder. Asking her for anything wasn't the easiest thing in the world. Not to mention her wardrobe ran much further to the super-feminine end of fashion than Pip liked. She didn't want to end up dressed in a forest-green ball gown.

Relaxing for the moment in contentment, Piper thrilled at the lights, textures, and shapes unfolding before her. She felt warmer than last time. And the air, instead of burning her nose with cold, smelled faintly sweet. A bit like apple pie. The world out here amazed and delighted her.

The feeling helped balance the dread of returning to Fitch's foster home. She kept telling herself she'd be there to free her Merry Band, but dread of rejection, fear of being laughed at, and terror of having to return to the Neverland with no back-up team at all, kept souring her stomach.

Approaching Seattle's nighttime skyline was incredible. The view banished her nerves, if only temporarily. Once, long ago with her parents, Pip remembered riding one of the Washington State Ferries at night toward downtown Seattle. The city lights reflected in the water of Puget Sound had been a sight to behold.

Seattle from the sky was twice as good. Beaming faintly through the mist, the lights seemed to be reflected not only by the surrounding water, but also by the cloud cover. The fuzzy glow almost made the place look warm and friendly.

Pip had to smile. Only someone from Seattle could say mist looked friendly. The moist air refreshed her face. She didn't even mind that she was kind of soggy by the time they circled the Space Needle, swooped over Lake Union, and cut over the humming freeway to Capitol Hill.

Tension grew in her tummy as they neared the foster home. They'd made a plan; time would tell if it would work.

Most of the buildings in this rainy city had pitched roofs, either slight, or more extreme. The foster home was an exception. The tar-covered roof lay just below them, flat as a pancake. Probably leaky as a sieve as well, Pip thought ruefully. But it made a perfect landing place for the dugout canoe.

Belle jumped off the prow while they were still airborne. Pip watched her bring the boat behind her to a halt with a touch of her tiny hand. The fairy descended and the boat followed. They landed with a bump. Pip climbed out, stowing her paddle in the hull with the others. She tiptoed to the roof's edge. Belle flew alongside.

They walked all the way around the rooftop, scoping out the lay of the land below. Pip looked for any obvious changes since she'd left with Belle. Sure enough. On the cement stoop at the front of the house, someone sat in a lawn chair, umbrella propped to keep off the wet night air. A security guard.

"We need to find out if he or she is armed," Pip whispered. She wore her dagger tucked through her belt, but she hoped not to have to use it. Somehow, the idea of wielding it against a regular person felt different than planning to slay pirates with it in the Neverland.

"All right. Can you climb down?" Belle asked. "I'm out of pixie dust. I can't fly you, even by the belt loop."

"Sure I can. The fire escape is over there." Pip gestured toward one side of the house. She'd seen it that first day when Miss Henning brought her. It passed in front of what she was pretty sure was Fitch's bedroom window, making it a bit tricky. Of course the old biddy had arranged things so the emergency escape was on her side of the house and not the foster girls'. "Meet you at ground level," she said to Belle in a low voice.

Carefully, she eased herself over the roof's edge, grabbing the cold ladder. Simple enough. She descended past the attic. Her foot reached from the last rung to the landing's iron grating. Busy peering down at Fitch's window, she miscalculated the distance. She landed with a metallic thump. Regaining her balance, she flattened herself against the house's wet siding, hardly daring to breathe.

She stared at the window just below. No movement. A siren shrilled and Piper froze. She prayed Fitch hadn't made a 9-1-1 call. The station was seconds away by patrol car—they'd never pull off the rescue if police or firefighters came. The siren faded. She breathed a sigh of relief and got ready to move again.

Crossing her fingers, she tiptoed across the landing and onto the section of ladder that would take her past Fitch's window. She silently counted each step down. *One, two, three*—

"What in the dragon's name is taking you so long?" Belle's loud whisper came from behind.

Pip jumped and half-turned. Her dagger clanged against iron. Fitch's window loomed beside her. She couldn't stop now. Down, down she moved, trying to keep quiet, but too scared to slow down. The ladder ended six feet above the ground. Pip jumped, landing in a bone-jarring crouch.

Scurrying to the front corner of the building, she ducked under the low branches of a huge rhododendron, ignoring the sting as its branches scraped her back. She looked up and thought she saw the flash of a white nightgown in the window. "Why'd ya scare me that way?" she hissed at Belle.

The fairy shrugged as if she didn't care.

Pip made a disgusted noise. "All right then, Miss Know-it-all. Did you see if the guard is armed?"

Belle nodded. "A holstered gun and a little black thing on his belt. He looked like he might be napping though."

Little black thing, little black thing ... Pip thought hard. "Oh. That's probably a cell phone. We'll have to get that too."

The foster home faced a city park. Like any park in a big city, the bodies of sleeping homeless people littered the benches and filled semi-dry nooks. Any one of them might be alarmed by her night prowling. She took some small comfort in the thought that most of those slumbering forms were probably drunk. Tonight that would be helpful. They wouldn't be easily woken.

One of the city's water-supply reservoirs lay fenced in the middle of the park. During daylight hours it had an aesthetic purpose: the center spurted water in the air—a poor substitute for a fountain. At the moment, it would be a great spot to hide the security guard's weapons.

"If I get his gun and his phone, can you drop them in the water over there?" Pip asked.

"That should only take a fleck of pixie dust. I can manage."

"Did you bring the sleeping potion?"

Belle nodded, pointing to a tiny seashell stoppered with a bit of sea sponge, hanging around her neck. The spiders had woven the necklace to order.

Pip didn't know where Belle got the potion, but Belle said it worked like a dream. Only one or two drops on a person's lips put them into a deep sleep for a couple of hours.

"Great. You apply the potion, I'll get his weapons."

Together they worked their way around the rhododendron. The guard sat in the dim circle of the porch light. His head dropped slowly, then snapped up and repeated itself. Good. He was already sleepy. Pip gestured Belle forward. She followed in a low crouch, staying close to the building.

Pip saw the front room light go on. "Duck!" She flattened herself beside a tall, skinny, evergreen shrub. The window curtains pulled back and a face peered out. It was Fitch. Darn it. She'd woken the old biddy. Pip suppressed a groan.

After several seconds, Fitch disappeared. Was she coming outside? Pip waited, expecting to hear the creak of the front door and Fitch's cranky voice at any moment. The sharp clean scent of crushed evergreen needles filled her nostrils. She didn't dare wipe the drip of water forming at the end of her nose.

Nothing happened.

She couldn't wait forever. Pip stepped out from her hiding place, trying not to make the bush rustle. Belle's light twinkled from under the seat of the lawn chair. She noticed that the angle of the guard's umbrella hid his upper body from the lit window. Fitch hadn't seen the man's head. If she'd caught him napping, she'd be out here now for sure.

"Go!" Pip whispered. Belle's light flashed out from under the chair. Waiting a moment, Pip crept up the concrete slab and knelt behind the guard.

"I dosed him. He should be out in a second or two," Belle whispered, shoving the stopper back in the seashell.

Carefully, Pip reached for the man's holster. Gripping the butt of the gun, she eased it out. Leaning to his other side, she went for the cell phone snapped to his belt. Getting it was more difficult.

"Mmmph." The guard grunted.

Pip froze. But the guard's breathing returned to its thick and steady rhythm, rumbling into a snore. Pip quickly set the cell phone beside the gun. "As soon as you get rid of those, I'll need your help."

Belle shook her hair over the phone and gun. Pixie dust shimmered, and they floated up beside her, three times her bulk.

As Pip watched, the fairy's light flitted through the air, and hovered over the reservoir's dark water. The satisfying sounds of two splashes followed.

Pip noticed a soft wool scarf loosely knotted at the sleeping guard's neck. Borrowing it, she draped it around her own neck. It might come in handy later.

Belle reappeared at Pip's side. "That was fun. What's next?"

"We've got to get inside. I've no idea how. Everything is locked up tighter than a stuck lid." Pip's whisper rose in agitation. She ticked off the problems on her fingers. "The guard doesn't have house keys. Fitch probably didn't trust him to carry them. I could maybe break into Fitch's bedroom, or even the door on the roof to the attic, but I can't get back up the fire escape without someone to give me a boost. And Fitch is awake in there. Maybe she's already called the cops," she said, spreading her arms in a frustrated shrug.

Belle cocked her head for a moment. "Not yet, she hasn't. No sirens. How's your arm?"

"Huh?"

"Can you throw pretty well?"

"Sure I can!" Pip opened her mouth, ready to defend her pitching skills, but Belle cut her off.

"Get some pebbles and come on!" She whirled around the corner to the north side of the house.

Of course. Throw pebbles at the girls' dormitory. They didn't have time to track down Fitch and dose her with the potion. They had to risk it. Go straight to freeing her Merry Band. Pip sped to the gravel driveway and gathered a handful of pebbles. Half crouching, she darted toward a spot below the dorm window, as close to the neighboring house as possible.

Ping. She hit the window on her first try. But it took three more "pings" before a bleary-eyed face appeared. Flim and Flam shared the bunk nearest the window. It must be one of them.

Belle's light gleamed outside the window. The face inside plastered itself against the glass to better see her. Belle backed up, gesturing for whomever it was to open up. Hands fumbled with the latch, and it ground open.

Pip winced. Old, loud wooden windows. Luckily no screens or storm windows to contend with.

A child's arm reached out toward the pixie, followed by a head and torso.

"Hey, Flim! Or are you Flam?" Pip whispered as loud as she could.

"¿Qué?" The twin looked down. "I'm Flim. Pipsqueak? Is that you? Where've you been?"

"No time! Drop down the fire escape ladder for me!"

Having to meet the city's building code, Fitch had secured a rope ladder to the bunk bed closest to the window. It was a flimsy thing. Pip had a vision of the night, not so long ago, when she'd climbed down it on her way to the University Bridge. Unattended, it would make the metal bed drag to the window and Fitch would be on them in seconds.

The rope ladder piled up in the window, falling out when Flim shoved it.

"Hold on to the bed!" Pip reached up for the bottom of the rope. She had to walk herself up the wall, pulling with her arms, before she could cradle a foot in the first step.

"Get off!" Flim hissed.

Pip jumped back to the ground.

"I cannot hold the bed!" Flim leaned out, eyes wide.

"Wake up Pudge. And your twin. The three of you can do it." Pip waited what seemed an eternity.

She sent up prayers that Pudge would cooperate without opening her loud mouth. And that Flim and Flam wouldn't get distracted and start some poking, giggling game.

Finally, she got a thumbs-up sign from above. Pip started climbing again, ignoring the swinging motion, moving as fast as she could. When she got up to the window, Pudge's hand reached out and pulled her in.

"Thanks," Pip panted. She bent to catch her breath, sighting Belle hovering under a bunk bed.

"What's goin' on?" Pudge spoke, but Flim and Flam leaned in for the answer as well. "Where've ya been? What's the big idea expecting us to save your sorry butt?"

Pip shook her head. "No time now." She saw Pudge take a breath to argue, and broke in before the big redhead could object. "Look—you hardly know me, and have no reason to trust me, but *please* ... I can get all of us out of here. Please, just this once, do this without asking questions. Get your packs and wake the others."

As she spoke, Pip pulled the hem of her floppy sweatshirt away from her body and subtly beckoned Belle to hide under it. She knew the fairy held her sleeping potion at the ready.

Soon, the foster girls stood in the center of the

room, sleepy and disheveled, school packs slung on their backs.

"Do you have any clothes in there, or just school books? Because you won't need school books where we're going."

Most of the girls pulled books out, piling them on bunk beds. Midge made a face. "What if I want a book along?"

"Fine!" Pip kept glancing toward the door, expecting Fitch at any moment. "Bring what you want, just be sure you've got something to wear besides pajamas. And put on your shoes, okay?"

"Bissus Fitch bakes us carry clothes id our packs," Stinky whispered. "She says we should always be prepared."

"Huh." Pip gave a half-laugh. Seemed like Fitch was helping them out in her own way.

"Are we coming back?" It was one of the twins.

"I hope not," Pip said. "Not if you trust me and do what I say. I'll get you out of here, I swear." The promise of liberty seemed to convince them to do as she said.

"Fitch alert!" Midge warned. Footsteps sounded outside the dorm room.

"When she comes in, help me rush her back out into the hallway, OK?" Pip had barely finished asking when the door opened. The girls sprang at the entering form, small weights in the dark hurtling against the skinny old broad. Fitch staggered backward, falling on her rump.

Delighted, Pip leapt, pulled the scarf from her neck and shoved it into the foster mother's mouth, gagging her. "Belle?" The tickling inside her shirt told her the fairy was still there. "Time to dose Fitch. On three."

The woman's eyes widened to twice their usual size when Belle flew out from the neckline of Pip's shirt, and squawked when the fairy stood on her chin.

The Lifers gasped at the bright creature as well.

"Holy ... " Pudge began.

"One, two, three." Pip whipped the scarf off Fitch's mouth and Belle zipped in, seashell poised. When the pixie finished, the scarf went right back on. "Just until she falls asleep," Pip said. She had to admit, she kind of enjoyed the terrified look in Fitch's eyes. Just a little payback felt good. "Everybody, we're dragging her to her room."

They struggled, trying to pull her back down the hall by her arms, rending grunts and groans from their victim.

"Let's try by her feet." Once they'd conquered the challenge of swiveling a tall woman in a narrow hall, the going was easy.

"Do we have to lift her into bed?" Stinky asked.

"Nah. This is good enough." Pip looked at Fitch. She slept soundly now, even spread as she was, on the hard wooden floor. Her flannel nightgown bunched up at the hips from her hallway trip. Pip tugged it down a little and removed the gag.

"Why are you bothering?" Pudge asked, scornful.

Pip shrugged. It didn't seem right to leave her all akimbo, even for Fitch.

"We're getting out of here now, guys," Pip said. "I saw a door on the roof. How do we get to it?"

"Follow me," Midge said. Pandemonium ensued, but by moving with the general hubbub, Pip found herself walking up creaky old stairs to the attic, and to the rooftop doorway.

Unbolting it, Midge threw it open to the cool night air, and stepped onto the roof. The girls poured out, all talking at once.

Pip waved her arms in the air, trying to get their attention. "Hey, please, we're not safe yet." She pointed to the boat. "Everybody in. Two to a bench. Stow your packs and grab a paddle."

They looked at her like she was crazy. Pudge walked around the boat. "Are you nuts? Of all the cock-eyed, idiot things—"

Stinky was the first to do as Pip asked. She shoved

her pack under the middle bench, gripped a paddle, and looked up expectantly.

Midge shook her head. "Well, here goes nothing." She joined Stinky. "C'mon, Pudge," she directed. "Flim, you get in front, Flam, in back. "I know, I know," she said, when the twins looked alarmed at not sitting together. "Pudge, be a sport. Sit up front with one of them. Zonk can—hey! Where's Zonk?"

"We're missing Thumb, too," Pudge said, scowling. She did as Midge asked, though.

Pip led the other twin to the back bench, keeping one reassuring hand on her shoulder as she took her own place in the stern. "We'll pick them up from the dormitory window."

"Shove off, everyone, like this." Pip demonstrated, pushing the end of her paddle against the roof. The boat rose into the air.

"Oohs" and "aahs" followed from the girls.

"Holy … " Pudge said, for the second time in a handful of minutes.

"Row, everyone, all together!" Pip steered with her paddle as they swished into the gray dark of the city sky.

The girls pulled air until they bumped broadside against the open dorm window.

Pip climbed inside, searching until she found the culprits. Zonk had fallen back asleep. No surprise there. The girl had seemed like she'd never wake up, given a choice. Leaning over Zonk, Pip saw Thumb nestled beside her.

"Wake up, Zonk!" Pip shook the girl, hard. She was too big to carry. Eyes slowly opened, and with urging, she rose, moving like a sleepwalker. When she climbed through the window and joined the twin on the back canoe bench, she smiled as though still dreaming.

Pip shuffled through the two remaining backpacks, pulling out books, shoving in shoes and the clothes she found under the bed. She tossed the packs to Stinky and Midge, who stowed them wherever they could find space. Lifting Thumb, Pip settled the still-sleeping little girl low in the bow. She pushed the boat forward until she could climb in the stern once again. She signaled to Belle, who flew ahead, yanking them all in her wake.

"Here we go, girls! To the Neverland!" Piper shouted at full voice, not caring who heard. "Second star to the right, and straight on 'til morning!"

She imagined they made quite a sight paddling their boat through the mist-laden sky, pink no-pirates flag and all.

"In the books I've read about sword fighting, it never said you bend your knees that much," Midge said.

CHAPTER TWELVE

Pan and Belle at Loggerheads

"**Y**ou promised you'd learn to fly if I helped bring those girls to the Neverland," Belle accused in Trouble's ear.

The girls who were supposed to make up the Merry Band gaped at them with varying degrees of attention. It was early afternoon, and naptime as far as Belle was concerned. Trouble had roused them from bed that morning to do what she'd called rowing drills—not that going round and round in circles, calling each other names, and splashing water everywhere looked particularly like rowing drills— and had barely let them stop since.

"Not now." Peter's heir swatted her away and continued what she'd been doing for what seemed like hours. "As I was saying," she said, in what Belle had learned was her lecture voice, "knowing and using the basic sword fighting stance can be the difference between life and death."

The youngest girl, the chocolate-brown one with the long eyelashes, whom they called "Thumb," started to cry.

"Shhh," the older reddish-brown girl with two shoulder-length braids said. She picked up the littlest and held her on one hip while rubbing her own eyes with a fist.

"I don't think that's right," the pretty Asian girl with glasses, Belle thought her name was "Midge," said, sounding irritated.

"What do you mean?" Trouble was downright testy.

"In the books I've read about sword fighting, it never said you bend your knees that much."

"Well we're not learning from a book, are we?" Piper snapped. "I'm showing you the real thing."

Belle tried again, clearing her throat before saying in a low voice, "Why don't you give the poor kids a break and let me teach *them* to fly, since you're too stubborn."

Trouble flushed. Ignoring the jibe, she said to the group, "Look guys. I know you think of me as 'Pipsqueak,' the one who got caught trying to fly to the Neverland. But we're actually *in* the Neverland, now, and as it turns out, I'm *Piper Pan*. I'm *trying* to train you to be my Merry Band. Couldn't I get a little respect? I mean—I do know about sword fighting, I really do."

"Cut it out, will ya?" Pudge's voice boomed. She lifted a fist and shook it at the twins. "If either of you hit me with a spitball again, I'm gonna give you what for." Her red curly hair gave Belle a stab of longing for Peter, though this girl was twice his size.

Completely identical in clothing as well as features, the twins' shiny dark hair looked as if it had been cut around an upside-down bowl. Their cherub faces would fool any jury, and their attention spanned no longer than the blink of an eye for anything but each other. The only thing they seemed to have going for them was their marksmanship.

Dropping her head nearly to her chest, Trouble looked the picture of dejection.

Belle took pity on her. Ignoring Peter's heir's admonition to let her do the talking, she flew forward. "Why don't you all sit down over here and rest for a little while? You can introduce yourselves and help me get to know you," she said, using her sweetest tone.

A sound that reminded Belle of nothing more than elephant flatulence answered her. The girls began to giggle. Belle prepared to give them a piece of her mind when the smell hit her and she nearly gagged. "What ... ?" she managed.

"I'm sorry." The little blonde girl who needed some serious help in the grooming department stepped forward. "I didn't mean to, really I didn't."

"You never mean to." The tone of Midge's

voice made Belle think of a splinter shoved under a fingernail. "That's why we call her 'Stinky,'" she explained to Belle. "She farts like a sailor." Midge laughed.

Belle raised an eyebrow. "Have you ever heard a sailor fart?"

Midge looked less sure of herself. "Well ... no, I haven't."

"I have," Belle assured the know-it-all girl. "Sailor farts don't compare in the least to hers." She pointed to Stinky, who stepped closer, her pale face lighting up like a candle. "Why don't you start," Belle said. "Tell me your name, how old you are and anything else I should know about you."

Trouble grumbled behind her.

Belle ignored the protest.

"I'b Stingky," the blonde girl said, pushing her stringy hair out of her face. "By real dame is Sara, but dobody calls me that. I'm seben years old and I thingk you're the most beautiful fairy in the world."

Warmth filled Belle, and she blinked in surprise. "Why thank you!" She nodded, recovering. "Anything else I should know about you?"

The girl shrugged, her eyes on the ground.

She could be pretty with a good bath, and with clothes that didn't hang on her little frame, Belle assessed. "All right," she said aloud. "You may sit down, Stinky." She gestured to the ground where the other girls clustered. "Who's next?" she asked.

"I'm the oldest, I'll go." Pudge stood up, banging into the big brown girl on her way to her feet.

"Watch it!"

"Sorry," the redhead mumbled. "I'm Pudge." she said in a jovial voice, "I guess ya can see why I'm called that. I'm twelve. I'm not really an orphan. My mom had me when she was fifteen and then she ran off and left me with my grandma who didn't want me and neither did anybody else." She spoke in a rush and shrugged like it was no big deal. "They passed me around and then gave me away and I ended up at Fitch's." She sat down. "When's dinnertime?" she added, worriedly.

"Soon," Belle said, working to keep her face serene. There were so many children out there who'd needed finding and bringing to the Neverland. She'd only focused on the boys until now. "Who's next?"

The tall girl with the two braids stood. "I'm Zonker. Zonk for short. I'm eleven." She sat down again.

Belle blinked. "Why are you called 'Zonk'?"

"Because she sleeps all the time," Midge retorted.

"Show her your tattoo," Stinky urged.

Zonk rolled up her left sleeve and showed off a rose tattooed on her shoulder.

"Very nice," Belle said, trying not to look shocked. She'd thought only pirates wore tattoos. "Anything else?"

Zonk shook her head.

"Nothing about your parents?" Belle was afraid of the answer after Pudge's introduction. She didn't need to start feeling sorry for this lot. "Maybe you could tell me how you got to be that lovely shade of reddish-brown," she suggested. Skin color seemed like a safe topic.

One eyebrow flew up in response and one side of Zonk's mouth pulled back in a scowl.

Midge heaved a sigh. "Could we get on with it? I'll tell you. Her mother was Indian and her father was Black, but she never knew him."

"Just call me the Native Black. Or the Black Indian." Zonk snarled the words and glared daggers at Belle.

"Don't, though, 'cause that's not nice," Stinky whispered.

"All right," Belle said, taken aback. Apparently skin color wasn't a safe topic after all.

"Could we get back to work now, *please*?" Trouble's last word was full of sarcasm.

"I'm not through yet." Belle glared at Peter's granddaughter. "Don't you want me to get to know your *Merry Band*?" She used sarcasm in return, and

Trouble flushed. Back to business, Belle pointed to the know-it-all girl. "I think you're next."

"I'm Midge, I'm ten, and my parents *did* want me." She threw a superior look at Pudge and Zonk.

"How come you're here with us losers then?" Pudge blared.

Midge's lower lip wobbled. She lifted her chin and pushed up her glasses. "My parents were killed in a car crash when I was four."

"Oh," Belle said. "I'm sorry."

Midge sat again. She kept her face down, propped in her hands.

The twins stood, arms thrown around each other's shoulders.

"I'm Cecilia Ana Caterina, but everyone calls me Flim," one of them said.

"*Me llamo Juanita María Angelina,*" said the other, "but you can call me Flam." She traded a look with her twin. "*Somos idénticos.*"

"Yeah," Flim agreed. "We're identical. But once you get to know us you'll be able to tell us apart. Right guys?" She looked to the other girls for confirmation.

"Oh, sure," Pudge said, laughing.

"We're good with spitballs." The girl called Flim grinned. "Slingshots too." She looked to Trouble.

"Maybe we could use slingshots instead of swords, *sí*?"

Trouble, who leaned against the Never Tree watching, grunted. "Okay." She grinned. "Save me the headache of trying to teach you, right?"

Good, Belle thought. The kid's sense of humor hadn't left her completely. "And you?" she asked the littlest girl, the one with the gorgeous fringe of black eyelashes.

"I'm Thumb," the little one said, from her seat in Zonk's lap.

"What's that you have in your mouth?" Belle asked.

"Duh." Pudge rolled her eyes.

"She wasn't being serious, stupid," Midge hissed.

Thumb smiled at Belle, so Belle ignored the name-calling. "And how old are you?"

Four fingers were held aloft. The thumb stayed in the child's mouth.

"She's a good kid," Zonk said. "Just gets tired kinda easy."

"Like you?" Midge said pointedly.

Pudge reached over and smacked Midge's head.

"That's enough, everybody," Trouble said, stepping forward. "And now, *if* you don't *mind*, Belle," she said, elbowing her way center stage, "we have a lesson to cover. Why don't you vamoose, and we'll talk to you later."

"Does she have to go?" Stinky sounded stricken.

"Yes." Trouble meant business. Belle couldn't miss that tone of voice.

She waved at the lot of girls. "See you all later. Maybe when you're tired of fighting you can come get flying lessons from me." She hung around long enough to listen to the trills of excitement followed by Trouble's disgusted refusals before taking her leave.

She was sure she could have those girls in the air in a trice. The Lost Boys had never gotten the knack, but these just might be different. In spite of her negative opinion of girls, she was willing to lay odds on it. Oh, they'd fly all right. And she'd bet her favorite tiara there'd be some changes in the Neverland once they did.

Why just this morning, when she'd reluctantly trailed the dugout canoe's drunken progress along shore, she'd seen a salmon jump in their wake. *A salmon!* There hadn't been any salmon left even five years ago, when she'd left for the Crystal City.

At noon when she'd gone to collect honey from the beehive for lunch, she'd heard bees talking about the dandelions they'd found. Up until now, Faery's

Nook with its fairy-powered blooms had been the Neverland's only pollen source.

"Trouble should understand the importance of getting them all to fly," she fumed as she made herself scarce. "But no. The kid only cares about making them a 'cohesive fighting team.' Fighting, schmighting. She has her priorities completely backwards."

The next day, Belle confronted Trouble after lunch, as the girl climbed the Never Tree to fetch her wretched swords.

"Well?" Belle felt as if she might self-combust from sheer frustration.

"Well, what?" Trouble kept her eyes on the tree, choosing her hand and footholds with care.

"*When* are you going to set aside some time for *flying lessons?*" She could hardly contain her fury.

Trouble balanced on a limb and reached for the velour-wrapped swords. She shrugged as if it didn't matter in the least.

"Don't you dare take that attitude with me, missy," Belle seethed. "You're only here by my grace, and don't you forget it. That little band of yours, too. You owe me."

The look in Trouble's eyes when they met hers chilled Belle from wing tips to toes.

"Owe you? Oh, so that's it, is it? I'm supposed

to be grateful?" Trouble's voice, like Belle's, was low, but filled with equal intensity. "You think this is just a lark, planning to avenge my parents? This is *work*. When the work is done, then maybe we'll have time to play your little flying games."

"Games?" Anger vibrated through her. "You don't know *anything*. Oh," she snarled, "if only Peter were here! *He* knew fighting only served if you were having fun. You just don't get it! What's really important is having a good time!"

Trouble looked at her like she was crazy. "A good time, huh? Well," she said, her voice cold, "I guess you'd know about *that*, wouldn't you?" And she climbed down, leaving Belle steaming.

The other girls wandered about below—each after her own end. Midge sat against the Never Tree, reading a book. Zonk napped next to a fallen birch, Thumb curled up beside her. The twins were having a slingshot marksmanship contest, aiming for Midge's book. Pudge, with Stinky in tow, collected firewood. Pudge wanted to build a bonfire later, and Trouble had agreed, possibly just to get Pudge to be quiet. Didn't Trouble realize the smoke and the glow of the flames would allow Li'l Jack and his men to track them?

"Well, I'm not going to warn them." Belle muttered. "What happens to them is their own doing."

As usual, talking aloud to herself made her feel a little better. She'd taken enough responsibility for this lot. Let them keep on like they were. The pirates would make short work of them—if they lived that long, if they didn't kill each other or themselves first. Trouble was off her rocker. These girls were the least likely team she'd ever seen. Grudging cooperation might be possible, but teamwork? Never.

"Girls are just plain silly," she growled as she flew off into the light brown afternoon air.

The Nook would be a much more welcoming spot than this girl-camp was turning out to be. She'd dress up, put on her most dazzling tiara, and try to think of some other clever plan to revive the Neverland. A plan that didn't involve a stubborn kid and her gaggle of girls.

"Oh, Peter," she cried as she flew. "They've moved into your Underground Home. Not Trouble, thank goodness, at least that stubborn runt has kept to her hammock in the Never Tree. But the others have taken it over! They've assigned themselves each a hollow tree entrance, and they act like they belong there!" she wailed. "Oh, I wish they'd all just go away. And how I wish *you* were here!"

Belle heaved a sigh. "But you aren't here, are you?" That was the whole point. "If you were here none of this mess would have happened. I'd still be *your* fairy. I'd never have needed to adopt Li'l Jack. I'd still be young and beautiful. And Sincoraz, that awful dragon, would still be wherever it came from." She shuddered, thinking of the beast and the havoc it wreaked.

"There has to be *some* way I can solve this problem by myself." Li'l Jack had let her down, and it seemed Trouble was shaping up to be just as unworthy of her trust. "A fairy should know better than to pin her hopes and dearest dreams on humans," she admonished herself. "What has trusting gotten me? Nothing but wrinkles."

Faery's Nook and its patch of green beckoned just ahead. "Oh, good," Belle sighed. She flicked her wings, hoping to revive the numb tips, and prepared to land on her bedroom balcony. "I'll go in, turn on my bubble-blower and make the world go away." An off-white paper fluttering next to her balcony stopped her mid-air. A note. It had to be from Li'l Jack. Trouble didn't know where she lived.

Settling, Belle inspected the paper. She admired its high quality, feeling its heavy texture before reading, in Jack's loopy script:

Dearest Godmother,

Please dine with me tonight in my quarters—the chef is preparing all your favorites. It will be my pleasure to celebrate your cleverness in finding Peter Pan's heir.

You were right all along—the Neverland needs Pan. I have been a fool. I beg your forgiveness. I am eternally and humbly yours,

Your prodigy godson,

Captain Li'l Jack

Post Script: I will await your presence onboard the Jolly Roger at moonrise.

Belle stared at the note. Suspicion shivered momentarily through her, but she brushed it away. "Hmph," she snorted. "Finally, the silly boy has seen the light. I'll enjoy nothing more than pointing out his folly." She shrugged. "And there's absolutely no harm in soaking up a bit of flattery at the same time."

Her eyes moved to her closet like iron to a magnet. She tapped her lip with her index finger. "The only question is," she mused, "what to wear?" She swept inside with a flourish. Presenting herself was what she did best.

✝

Piper and the Lifers sat around the remnants of their bonfire. Its smoldering coals lit their faces in an orange glow. Darkness, thick as day-old macaroni and cheese, clung everywhere but inside their circle. Several pairs of eyelids drooped. They'd actually been having a good time. There had been some argument over who got to do what, when, but they'd been singing, dancing, and telling tales for hours.

"But Pipsqueak, why can't we learn to fly?" Pudge whined. I've been living on spring water and honey. I think I deserve a break."

"You haven't been hungry, have you?" Piper pointed out.

"No, but why should you be the only one getting what you want?" Pudge thrust out her lower lip and folded her arms across her chest.

"Yeah." Zonk suppressed a yawn.

"Belle keeps asking us to do it," Midge pointed out. "She must be right. She's lived here a long time."

"Wight." Thumb snuggled up to Midge. Piper had noticed the child hadn't seemed to need her delicious friend nearly as much in the last couple of days, nor had she been as fussy. She stuck it in her mouth now, though, and her eyes shuttered closed.

Pip frowned at Midge. "There isn't always just one 'right,' you know."

Midge made a face, and an unintelligible comment under her breath.

"There's no telling *you* that, of course," Piper grumbled.

"Where is Belle, anyway?" Stinky looked around hopefully.

Piper sighed. To Stinky, the fairy was a dream-come-true. The kid would love to be just like Belle, and everyone knew it. Piper felt an unexpected flash of jealousy. She wished she could inspire such devotion in someone.

"Dunno," Piper barked. She saw them all flinch, and softened her tone. "Look, guys. It's either fight or flight, you know what I mean? It's my job to be sure we're good at the fighting part. It won't help us when we meet the pirates if all we can do is fly away."

She looked around the campfire at the glum faces. Getting to her feet, she stretched and yawned. "Okay, everybody, it's bedtime. We've got an early start tomorrow. Rowing at sunrise."

"Aaww, do we have to?" Groans of protest sounded, but the girls got to their feet.

It's still hard to think of them as a Merry Band, Piper thought.

"Night, Pipsqueak," Pudge mumbled.

"See ya tomorrow." Zonk yawned and gathered Thumb from Midge's lap into her arms.

"Sleep tight," Stinky called.

"Don't let the bedbugs bite." Pip watched her troupe disappear into the Underground Home, each through her own hollow-tree entrance, except the twins, who shared one. They all swore the entrances fit as if designed for them.

She wished they'd start calling her "Piper Pan," or even just "Pan," instead of "Pipsqueak," but she knew she had to prove herself worthy to be their leader. True, she'd helped them to liberty, but this place was barren, dusty, and ugly, never mind cursed by a person-inhaling dragon. They'd made no effort to hide their disappointment. Pudge wanted food, Midge a library, Zonk a comfortable bed, Stinky to be Belle's best friend, the twins to be left alone to their own devices, and Thumb—Piper sighed. She didn't know what Thumb wanted.

Still, she was actually in *the Neverland*. Even more, miracle of miracles, she was Peter's heir. "I'm Piper Pan now," she said softly. A thought sent the corners of Pip's mouth down. "I still can't fly." How could the girls call her Piper Pan when she couldn't fly? Oh well. She let the worry go. Tomorrow was another day.

She climbed the Never Tree to her hammock and made herself comfortable. The stars shimmered faintly overhead, as if they belonged in another world. The strong scent of wood smoke stung her nose. It smelled good. Tonight had been fun, if chaotic. Piper smiled. The girls had earned some fun. They'd been working hard. They were nowhere near a fighting team, but she couldn't deny they were trying.

They'd be happier still if she gave them a day with Belle to learn to fly. She knew she'd promised the fairy to learn herself. Piper winced. She'd just pretended it wasn't important this afternoon when Belle confronted her. But the old pixie had been nothing but snotty since their return.

First things first, Pip thought. Obviously, the girls' fighting skills weren't so hot. Their sword work was really awful. Piper had started at two years old, with a soft sword toy and gentle lessons from her mother. She'd forgotten how much repetition was required before the movements came naturally. Right now, if they met armed enemies they'd be hacked to pieces.

"Maybe they should learn to fly soon," she said to the stars, and snorted softly. "My fighting band is going to need a way to keep out of reach."

She snuggled in and allowed her eyes to close. She slept so much better here. Even the empty ache of knowing she'd never see her parents again didn't keep her awake long.

"T'morrow," Pip muttered. She'd make arrangements with Belle tomorrow. No doubt it would cheer the fairy up loads to teach her someday-to-be Merry Band to fly.

CHAPTER THIRTEEN

Trapped

Flea and the two burly men he'd ordered to accompany him stood at the edge of the large clearing around the Never Tree and its circle of hollowed out snags. They'd rowed up the coast to Cannibal Cove, taken the first bend of Crocodile Creek, and portaged inland to cache the rowboat at the origin of Kidd's Creek. Ready transportation for four: three pirates and one captive.

A glance at the stars told him midnight approached. The perfect hour for a bit o' mischief. This should be easy. He grinned and stared at the tree's dim bulk.

The barest light came from a slightly smoking pile of coals. Campfire remains. He'd seen the blaze from a distance, on the journey here. What one li'l girl needed with a fire that size, he'd no idea.

In the tree above, hung the slim hammock he'd spotted on his last trip here. The girl slept up there. Peter Pan's heir, the captain had said. Flea crossed his fingers behind his back to ward off evil. The flying lad in green had been nothing but trouble. But this li'l lass couldn't be anything like him.

Eyeing the downed tree limbs they'd chosen as tools, Flea nodded to the other pirates. "All right, men," he whispered. "Accordin' to the plan. Mind ye, be quiet. The scurvy li'l fairy should be aboard the *Jolly Roger* with the cap'n, but in case she's 'ere, we doesn't want to wake her."

They made their way across the clearing. Flea held up his hand to halt the procession each time one of them stepped on a twig or a pinecone. When all remained quiet, they tiptoed on. At last they reached the base of the tree.

With silent direction from Flea, the two burly pirates each raised one end of their tree limb into the air until it touched an end of the hammock.

Either this will work, or the hammock will come tumblin' down, Flea thought. "Steady," he breathed. Sure enough, just as he'd hoped, the sticky spider webbing stuck to the limbs, effectively severing the hammock from the Hollow Tree. "Down we go. Easy," He gestured with both hands, palms down, in case his barely spoken command hadn't been heard.

The men lowered their load, equalizing the weight hand over hand as it dropped. Flea held his breath while the hammock settled to the ground, like a leaf landing on water. The girl slept on. He stepped closer and looked at the child lying on her back, completely unaware of her situation. Signaling the others to move in with rope, he pressed a broad palm over her mouth.

The girl woke at his touch, eyes wide and alarmed. She shouted beneath his muffling hand and flailed about. But she was no match for three pirates. In moments, they had her gagged and bound.

"Might as well use the 'ammock t' carry her t' the boat," Flea whispered. His two companions hefted the load to their shoulders, grumbling at the sticky sensation.

"Quiet," Flea growled. They'd accomplished their mission, but it just seemed right to be quiet on a night like this. Leaning over the girl, he smoothed her hair. She jerked away. "See 'ere now, li'l miss," he said. "Ye're in good 'ands. Go back t' sleep, why don't ye. We've a bit of a trip ahead of us."

†

Piper grit her teeth around the nasty gag in her mouth. It tasted of sweat and fish guts. She'd no doubt they were taking her to Captain Li'l Jack. Misery dragged at her like a sinking stone. She'd allowed herself to be caught, unarmed and unaware.

None of the girls would know what had

happened to her. Although she'd shown them the general direction of Kidd's Cove and the *Jolly Roger*, they didn't really know where it was. Of course, it would take some time for them to be concerned at her absence. Her connection to them was still so tenuous. She couldn't be sure they'd come after her at all.

If they came for her, they'd walk right into a trap, sure as she lived and breathed. Actually, she should say "sure as she lay curled in the wet hull of a rowboat, bound and gagged." Who knew how long she'd live and breathe? One good thing: they were on the water, traveling downstream—the boat fairly purred, no tossing as it would on the ocean. They were probably on Kidd's Creek. Which meant they weren't traveling to the dragon's lair. At least not yet.

She needed to buy herself some time. Belle would show up at camp tomorrow wanting to teach the girls to fly. The fairy would figure out what had become of Piper, or "Trouble," as she insisted on calling her. She would tell the girls to stay put.

Belle had said children weren't ripe enough for Sincoraz's taste, but Piper wasn't so sure. If the beast was hungry enough, it would probably eat anything. Pip shuddered. Very little remained alive on the Neverland. Just a crew of smelly pirates, an old pixie, some insects, and now Pan and her not quite

Merry Band. Unfortunately, the latter would be the sweetest choice.

She wouldn't have the destruction of those girls on her hands. They might not be her friends yet, but she was responsible for bringing them here. Nothing terrible could happen to them. She'd do anything to stop that.

Obviously, the pirates took her for easy bait. She flushed as she realized that's exactly what she'd been. All she could do now was play on their assumptions. She lay in the creaking rowboat, stared at the faint faraway stars, and tried frantically to think of a plan.

†

Captain Li'l Jack glanced out his porthole. The moon's round face peered back, already floating well above the choppy horizon. She was late. Not that that should surprise him. Tiny though she might be, Belle was every inch a lady. And a lady always takes her time.

He checked the table for the umpteenth time. Gold flatware shone, reflecting the soft light of a dozen lit candles. The white linen tablecloth set off the crystal glassware and china plates. Belle's place setting mirrored his, in miniature. He'd ordered them made long ago, when they first celebrated his captaincy. He'd still been but a boy. Her woven rattan chair, cushioned with down, hung suspended from the ceiling at just the right height.

Sometimes when they shared a meal, he set her place on a miniature table in the birdcage and hung it close by so they could dine at eye level. But tonight he preferred she have to look up to meet his eyes.

"Perfection," he gloated aloud. Unconsciously he sharpened his hook on the steel of his claw-arm. "She'll fall for it hook, line, and sinker." His brow furrowed. "As long as she received my invitation … " If she'd only been with Peter's heir at the Never Tree since she'd last been here, there was a chance she'd missed it.

As if in answer to his concern, the tinkle of bells sounded outside the porthole. Belle's light glowed, eclipsing the moonlight. The captain let her in with a bow. "Welcome, my dearest godmother. I'm so glad you could join me. You look absolutely exquisite."

He didn't have to pretend about that, anyway. She wore a gown of white iridescent feathers, exceeded in their delicate shimmering only by her magical fairy wings. Emerald jewelry sparkled, lending splendor to her sparkling eyes. Her hair might be a shade less fiery than when she'd been young, but hardly noticeably. Crowning it all, a diamond tiara rested on her pixie head.

Looking away, Li'l Jack coughed to cover his smile. He'd learned his pretensions from a master. "That's what I'd call 'gilding the lily,'" he said with a straight face.

"Do I, or do I not know how to dress for a celebration?" Belle posed, arms extended, awaiting his compliment.

"You do indeed," he said. It certainly was a pity she'd traded away the bloom of her youth, he thought. At one time, she'd appeared more like an older sister beside him than the grandmother she was now.

A fairy-sized sister, of course but when it came to beauty, a pirate captain needed a showy woman at his side. Belle had always served. Size simply didn't matter when it came to her. But since she'd traded away those twenty years, her looks only reminded him of his own dreaded future.

Bah, he thought, I'm in my prime. Old age is a long way away. Staring at Belle, his longing for affection and approval rose unbidden. "I've missed you," he blurted, and then regretted it. Blast it all— he needed to be the one in charge tonight.

"Of course you have." Belle smiled and curtsied low. "I've missed my little boy Jack."

Realizing his admission could be used to his advantage, he relaxed. "Please, my dear godmother."

He inclined his head, directing her to her seat with a flourish. "I'm so looking forward to our evening." If she only knew how much.

He narrowed his eyes at the lines around her eyes and mouth. If it weren't for the dragon's hidden treasure, the Life Elixir, he'd have said Belle's trade wasn't worth it. Youthful beauty couldn't be matched by maturity, not in his eyes. But this was no time to point that out to her.

Their meal went on and on. The food was divine, the service silent and expedient. The ship's larder had been newly stocked. During a recent raid for Sincoraz, he'd pillaged the kitchens of the well-to-do along with their homeowners.

Caviar, champagne, salmon mousse. French onion soup, filet mignon, roasted guinea hens. Asparagus, butternut squash, *petit pois*. Raspberry mint sorbet, *crème brûlée*, and chocolate mousse. Not to mention wines selected for each course, ending with a brandy for him and a tiny glass of port for her.

He fairly salivated knowing all this was only an appetizer. A teaser for the delight yet to come. "Remember the time I loosed bubonic plague on that ship of prisoners?" he chuckled.

"How could I forget? You rubbed spoiled meat on the lines, slung them over, and the rats poured aboard." She purred the words. He'd refilled her wine glass liberally. "You didn't even offer—hic—to let them join your crew."

"I did you proud that day, did I not?"

"You've always done me proud, you handsome devil." Her eyelids drooped, flying at half-mast.

"Oh, the times we had." He raised his glass. "Let's drink to them. And to us. Godmother and godson." He watched her toss the liquor back in one gulp while he merely sipped his own.

"Why'd they ever stop? Those good times?" she asked. "Why didn't you leave well enough alone with that—hic—that dragon? Why did you have to become its keeper and feed it people and let the Neverland—hic—be ravaged? Why," she glared with all the fierceness a drunken fairy can summon, "wasn't I more important to you?"

"That's what I wanted to say tonight." Li'l Jack fluttered his eyelashes at her, knowing she was too far gone to think it odd. "Belle, I've been blind. I should never have let you go. A boy always needs his mother. I want you to come back. Please, be the queen of my realm. Look after me like you always have."

Belle blinked, confusion on her face. "I—hic—I can't. How can I come back to a son who is destroying my—hic—my world?"

"Oh, Belle," Li'l Jack got down on one knee. "I'll give it all up for you." He gloried in the sheer melodrama of his performance. He amazed himself. Nothing short of award-winning. "Me hands mean *nothing* compared to you. I thought they were my dream, but no! You are my dream! My Belle, my own fairy godmother!" Oh, he could retch. How disgusting.

Belle positively melted. "My dear little Jack. Bring my world back to life, and we'll—hic—we'll find another way to get you hands. We'll storm—hic—the seas and steal booty enough to buy you the best." She sank in her chair, askew, but unable to fully right herself.

"I have a gift for you to seal our new partnership. But you must sit up here to receive it." Standing, Li'l Jack leaned across the table and scooped Belle up on one finger. He carried her to the cage and set her inside on the elegant daybed. He reached into his armoire and brought out a jewel-encrusted net of tiny gold chain-link.

"What is it—hic?" she asked. "It's beautiful. It looks like a tent for a queen."

"Ah, me bright beauty, it is! I designed it for the Nook. It will cover yer sweet little castle, and ye'll be able to see out, but no one can see in. Protection fit for royalty."

"O—hic—oh," she gasped, eyes wide.

"Would you like to try it?" He couldn't control his grin.

"Of course." She crossed her long fairy legs and clasped her hands in her lap, waiting in anticipation.

Li'l Jack carefully laid the net over the cage. It was long enough to gather together underneath. Pulling the velvet ribbon from his hair, he knotted it tightly.

"Ye can see out, can't ye, milady? But I can't see ye at all." He laughed, a musical sound if he said so himself. He'd done it. He'd trapped the wrinkled little broad. She was his to do with as he pleased. She couldn't stop his plans now.

†

"It's marvelous!" Belle sighed. She felt as if she were inside a treasure chest. The golden veil dimmed the light a bit, but what came through from the kerosene lamp and the candles still burning on the table shimmered and sparkled.

A tickle of desire, inspired by the gold and jewels, swelled. She stretched out a hand to touch the precious stuff, but it hung out of her reach. All she had to do was rise to her feet and stroll a few paces, but at the moment it seemed far too difficult. Instead, she giggled with pleasure, knowing her prodigy had grown up to be not only ingenious, but generous as well. He would always treat her in the royal manner she deserved.

Belle attempted to suppress a yawn, but it won the battle. "Aahhmmmm." She felt so very tired, and when she moved, everything seemed to spin. From very far away, she heard a voice.

"Ship ahoy! Request permission to come aboard wi' the prisoner, Cap'n."

She knew that voice. It belonged to a mutt of a man. Flea, wasn't it? She needed to sit up, to pay attention. What prisoner could he be bringing aboard at this hour?

She shook her head. Her eyes wouldn't stay open, and her body felt like seaweed, adrift on a vast ocean. Belle tried to follow the line of thought, but it kept dividing, arcing like a rainbow, and finally dissolved completely into gray mist.

CHAPTER FOURTEEN

Betrayed

S he would do her best to play the part of a meek and cooperative prisoner. All the same, while the pirates trussed her up to be hoisted aboard, Piper managed to give one pirate an elbow in the throat and the other a header to the groin.

"Ugh!"

"Ooof!

"I'm so sorry," she lied through the gag. She faked an apology with her eyes. "Clumsy me!" Of course the pirates only heard "Ah-o-orry," and "uh-y ee."

Fear curled in her belly as the rope and pulley lifted her onto the main deck. Better to show fear than fury. She kept her eyes wide while a pirate with one wooden leg loosed the ship's rope.

"Untie her feet as well, man." The weird, wild-eyed one spoke. He'd been in charge of her capture. He'd given the orders and the other two lugs had carried them out. "I'll take her down to the cap'n's quarters. She'll be no trouble 't all."

"Aye aye, sir." Pirate One-Leg saluted sharply

before leering at her. "Bit young for the cap'n, i'n't she?"

"Mind yer business," Her captor snarled. "Unless ye want a touch o' the hook or claw, ye swab?"

"No sir!" The pirate bent to his work, his head shaking back and forth like a Ping-Pong ball.

As the rope binding her feet fell to the deck, Piper considered bolting. Then she heard the clunk of heavy feet behind her. The two lugs. She wouldn't get far if she ran.

"Get back down there and ready the rowboat to be hauled aboard, ye snail-brained fool," one snarled.

"Don't tell me what to do, ye blitherin' ijit," replied the other.

The arguing voices faded as Pip stumbled below deck, dragged by her bound hands. Her crazy-looking captor glanced back at her from time to time with a funny expression. Maybe he was trying to be friendly. But with those eyes he just looked like a total kook.

She kept her own expression one of frightened innocence, letting neither the disgust nor the desire she had to pop him one show on her face. She wanted to spit, and gouge what nails she had into pirate flesh. But that wouldn't help. She needed to be smart here—to pay attention and watch for the right opportunity.

Her captor came to a halt and knocked three times on a wooden door. The captain's quarters, she presumed.

"Come." It was the captain's voice. She recognized it from the shocking scene her first day here, when he'd led that load of terrified men to Sincoraz and their doom. Not to mention from the night he'd kidnapped her mother and father. But this time his tone was slick with syrupy glee.

The door swung open and she was pushed inside. The captain sat facing her on the far side of the cabin, in a red velvet armchair. It set off his white shirt, black pants, shiny black boots, his faded mane of hair, blue eyes, and shiniest of all, the steel hook and claw resting where his hands ought to be.

"Welcome to me quarters." Captain Li'l Jack inclined his head with pretended good manners.

Piper didn't move, but glanced around, taking in the richly appointed quarters. A massive four-poster bed curtained with blue velvet dominated one side. On the opposite wall stood a table—the captain had dined in style. She'd never seen such fancy plates and silverware. Her mouth watered at the smells of food. Candles burned low; it must have been a romantic dinner for two. To the captain's left hung a golden jewel-covered thing. Was it a lampshade?

Behind the table in the corner stood a massive

wooden armoire—truly a wardrobe through which to reach Narnia, Pip thought, with a twitch of humor. Imagine, the White Witch and Captain Li'l Jack allied. She dismissed the idea. Aslan would send the captain running in terror with a single roar.

But the captain wasn't running now, far from it. He smirked at her from his throne. Rising to his feet, he moved with the grace and power of a panther.

She had to look up to meet his eyes. She waited like a frightened rabbit for him to pounce. Courage, Pip, she thought. Remember, you're Piper Pan. She tried to swallow. Her dry throat couldn't manage.

He laughed and took a step toward her. "I don't believe we've been properly introduced. Me name is Captain Li'l Jack. I am captain of the *Jolly Roger* and the Scourge of the Seven Seas and beyond. This," he gestured to her captor, "is me First Mate, Flea."

Her captor bowed. "Pleased t' meet ye."

"Shut up, Flea!" the captain snapped. "When I want ye to say something, I'll tell ye." Looking back at Piper, he cocked his head to one side, eyes narrowing. "I understand we should have met already. How many years ago was it?" He smirked.

It took all of Piper's will power to remember she wasn't supposed to have been there the night he robbed her of her parents. She'd been huddled in her closet. She could still hear her father's voice saying, "Our niece sometimes sleeps here. We have no children of our own." She wrinkled her brow at the captain as if to say: "We should have?"

Waving his claw with impatience, the captain said, "She can't pay her respects that way, Flea. Take off her gag at once."

The loose lacy cuff of the pirate captain's sleeve revealed a flash of steel forearm, sending a shiver up Piper's spine. Flea untied the filthy gag. She coughed. The taste in her mouth revolted her. "May I please have a drink of water?" Oh good, she thought, I sound as meek as any sorry orphan.

The captain raised an eyebrow. "Well, our guest is a little lady, I see. Bring her some water, Flea."

Flea headed to the romantic table, still trimmed with half-filled glasses and plates boasting yummy-looking food. He reached for a water glass.

"Not that water, you fool!" the captain snarled. "Get some from the galley."

"Aye aye, Cap'n." Flea saluted and fled, shutting the door behind him.

The captain circled her, hook and claw behind his back.

Piper straightened under his critical gaze.

"Who'd have thought Pan would spawn such a mangy child?" He spoke quietly, each word a weapon.

Piper refused to flinch. She wouldn't take the bait.

"The flying boy was a scurvy brat," he continued, "but you, my dear, look like a cowardly sparrow. Plain as a catfish and skinny to boot. Peter Pan made a fool of Hook. He baited the croc, gave the beast a taste of the good pirate's flesh. It stalked him and finally ate him alive." The captain completed his inspection. He stared down at Piper, blue eyes smoldering. "But there's no croc now, and I'm not Hook."

She couldn't help herself, the words blurted out. "No croc, maybe, but there is a dragon."

The captain grimaced. Eyes narrowed, mouth tight, he looked nothing short of deadly.

At that moment, the cabin door burst open and Flea stumbled in. "Here's the water, Cap'n. Want that I give it to the girl?"

Piper reached for the glass without waiting for permission. Gripping the water with both hands, as her wrists were still bound, she drained the contents without stopping. When she handed the glass back to Flea, she let out a loud belch. The First Mate blinked and backed up against the wall awaiting further orders. Piper's eyes returned to the captain's.

He curled his lip. "Ah, so that's how it is. The sparrow has a song after all. Much like a crow."

Captain Li'l Jack half-turned his head, speaking over one shoulder. "Isn't that so, Belle?"

Belle? Piper stared in confusion. *Belle? Here?*

Catching her look, the pirate captain laughed. "Ye didn't know, did yeh? Of course she's here. Belle and I are partners. I'm the pirate king, and she's the fairy queen." He gestured toward the golden lamp-like thing suspended from the ceiling.

"She's sitting on her throne, in there, watching you. Aren't you Belle?" Leaning in, he tried to peer inside the roundish gold thing. That must not have worked because he pressed an ear against it and cleared his throat. "Belle?"

An odd sound like a faintly buzzing bee came from the golden shape. A tinkling, buzzing bee.

Captain Li'l Jack made a noise in his throat like an angry goat. Undoing the tie at the bottom of the thing, he pulled the bejeweled cover up and off … of a cage.

Piper gasped. Belle lay on a miniature couch, the fancy kind she'd seen in antique stores, fast asleep. One arm hung over the side and her shoes were kicked off. The dainty high heels made Pip think of Cinderella's glass slippers.

"You've drugged her. You captured her and made her drink a sleeping potion." Pip spoke fast.

She sounded too young, too defensive, but she couldn't help it.

"Oh, no." He shook his head. His hair, hanging in soft waves, brushed his shoulders. "Not at all. She came of her own free will." His claw moved, pointing to the table. "She dined with me. She's only sleeping because she drank too much."

For the first time, Piper saw the size of the second place setting. Tinker Bell sized. The serving platters laden with food had kept her from noticing before. A teeny chair hung suspended from the ceiling like a porch swing. Belle *had* dined here. Piper felt a lump in her throat. She kept her mouth shut, but her head shook back and forth of its own accord.

"Yes, me pretty Pan. Belle is not your savior. Let me tell ye about your pixie friend." He gave a mean bark of laughter. "Well. Not actually *your* friend. *My* friend? Yes. Your friend? I'm afraid not. Would ye care to sit down while I enlighten yeh?" Standing tableside, he offered the human-sized chair.

Piper shook her head.

"No? Well then." *Clang.* The horrid man whipped his hook onto a plate, spearing a piece of meat.

Piper started at the sudden movement and the sound of steel on china.

"Hungry?" He extended it to her and laughed when she refused. "Then I'll help meself." The hook lifted to his lips in slow motion, and they accepted the offering.

Piper shuddered.

Clang. This time the hook speared a piece of asparagus. "As I was saying, Belle and I have quite a history." He strolled back to the red armchair and sat while his hook fed him the long green vegetable as if it were a spaghetti noodle. Wiping his mouth on his sleeve, he continued. "I am Belle's protégé."

Hope drained from Piper like air from a pricked balloon. Who would help her now? And who would keep the Merry Band safe from harm?

"In a sense, I am Peter Pan's successor."

CHAPTER FIFTEEN

Condemned

"In a sense, I am Peter Pan's successor." Captain Li'l Jack held up his hook to silence her "No, lest ye ask," he growled, "she didn't teach me to fly."

Pip hadn't been about to ask. It must be a sore point.

"But that was only because I never wanted to fly. Why would I want to be like that namby-pamby Pan? No. Flying is for birds and small boys." He leaned back in the chair, crossing one booted ankle over the other thigh. "As you can see, I'm not a small boy, but a man. A very, very powerful man." His hook tapped the boot's heel with each *very*. "Belle made me that way.

"Ye see—she's not on your side." He looked fondly up at the caged, tiny, sleeping form. "She doesn't care what happens to yeh. She doesn't care what happened to yer parents.

"Ye do know what happened to yer parents, don't yeh?" His voice was ever so soft, like a knife slicing silk.

She struggled to keep her face normal, but knew she paled at the memory of those people fading into nothing.

"I see ye do." He smiled. The gold crowns on his teeth shone.

He probably stole those crowns out of one of his victims' mouths, she thought.

"She cares about only three things," the captain continued. "Herself, the Neverland, and me. Not necessarily in that order." He winked at Piper.

Vile man. Pip was long past keeping a stony or innocent expression. She sneered, past caring how it affected her chances of escape.

"Perhaps she told ye we fought," the captain continued. "'Tis true." His hook wandered to his faint moustache, tracing the line from lip to goateed chin. "But not about me feeding humans to the dragon. Not about me ridding the world of Peter Pan's heirs—yer parents that is. I didn't know ye existed until recently. We fought because she's getting old."

The captain rose, walked to the cage and watched the snoring pixie for a moment in silence. "She knows she's going to die in due course, as all living things do, and she's grasping at straws to turn back the clock.

"Mind you, she brought it on herself." He

wandered to the table again. Clamping his claw onto a spoon, he loaded it with caviar and shoveled it into his mouth. "Mmmm. Sure ye wouldn't like some?"

Piper shook her head, feeling sick to her stomach. She had the most awful thought that he was telling her the truth.

"I'm sure she hasn't told ye this part of the story." He brandished the empty spoon at her, smiling like a kid with a secret. "The dragon—ye've met? Sincoraz. Belle wants ye to get rid of it. Am I right? I'd bet me ship and all me treasure she didn't tell ye how it came to be here in the first place."

He leaned toward Piper and whispered, as if they were partners in a conspiracy. "She summoned it." He stood tall again, nodding sagely. "She traded twenty years of her youth, in fact, for the summoning spell. 'Twas Belle who brought the curse down on the Neverland."

Piper's horror must have shown on her face. Every time she thought this couldn't get worse, it did. The evil man was telling her Belle called in the beast that had consumed her parents. That little pixie had pretended to be her friend. She'd cry right now if she weren't standing in this heartless pirate's cabin.

"Oh, yes! Ye see—I'd become captain of the *Jolly Roger*, as she and I had planned. She helped me gain victories no pirate had gained before or ever will after me. In fact, I'd beaten all me adversaries. Especially the ones in the Neverland. No Lost Boys left, no Indians left." He made a face and rolled his eyes. "Bor-ing!"

His expression returned to what she supposed was normal, and he continued. He was really getting into the swing of his story now. His cheeks glowed pink and his eyes sparkled. "Belle always preferred staying close to this wretched island. She'd get terribly homesick on long forays at sea. But she knew I'd no reason to stay here any longer. Not without challenges to meet. So she went about summoning a 'worthy opponent' for me, as she so aptly put it.

"She journeyed to the Fairy Kingdom, to the Crystal Palace itself. Of course the King and Queen of the Fairies, Oberon and Titania, wouldn't interfere with affairs of the Neverland. However, me clever fairy godmother found Pearl, a fairy known to dabble in Black Magic. Pearl gave her the spell in exchange for Belle's youth." He lifted his hook in victory. "She traded her beauty to keep *me*.

"Just like she's trading *you* to keep me. Ha, ha!" The pirate captain did a sort of jig while pointing at Piper. "She doesn't need ye anymore. And I certainly don't need yeh. Which is why ... Ffleea!" he bellowed.

Piper turned in time to see the First Mate jerk upright from his standing nap against the wall.

"Aye aye, Cap'n." He saluted so hard she heard the clunk of his head bouncing off the wall.

"I was just saying, Flea," Captain Li'l Jack's tone returned to soft syrup. "That the company of this fair—rather, *plain* maiden—is no longer required. How shall we dispense with her, Flea?"

Flea's eyes opened wide. "But Cap'n, she's just a slip of a girl. She might make a good scullery maid … " he trailed off at the captain's dark look. "I know, Cap'n! Ye shot the ship's boy last week. P'rhaps she could take 'is place?"

"NO, FLEA!" The glasses on the table quivered and two of the candles went out. One golden fork fell to the floor.

Flea rushed to pick it up.

"I said, Flea," the pirate purred, "How shall we dispose of her? DISPOSE! As in GONE FOREVER, FLEA!"

This time a knife and a crystal goblet crashed to the floor.

"C-C-Cap'n! Aye aye, Cap'n. How indeed, Cap'n?"

Li'l Jack grinned. "Now ye've the right of it, Flea. Hmmm. Let me see. Hanging? No. Too ordinary. Draw and quarter her? Oh, no. That's right. The last pirate I used the contraption on broke it. He was too tough to rip."

Sweat broke out on Piper's brow. She squeezed her hands together so their shaking would not be seen.

"We need something suited to a Pan. She can't be allowed to fly away, nor do we want her anywhere near a sword." The captain paced as he spoke, all the while eyeing his victim. "Of course we don't need to worry about a rescue, her fairy is quite incapacitated." He tossed the jewel-encrusted cover over the cage, retying the net.

"I know!" He walked up to Piper and bent his face close to hers.

Not so close that she could bite him, unfortunately.

"Death by drowning."

Piper's heart sank, and her mouth went dry. She resisted the temptation to squeeze her eyes shut. She didn't cry or plead. But she must've looked scared, because he looked delighted.

"Yes, that's it. The tide is just starting out now, Flea. It's what ... half past five in the morning?" He strode to the table. Lifting the cloth, he opened a drawer and consulted a chart. "The next high tide is at seven oh-two this evening. Sunset is at half six. Hmmm. I'd rather watch her drown in broad daylight, but twilight will have to do.

"All right, Flea!" He raised his voice in a command. "Take her out and stake her to the old pier. Be sure ye weigh her down with plenty of stones in her pockets. Tie some to her waist and ankles as well."

"But Cap'n, the ol' pier's still covered with water, Cap'n."

"When ... the ... water ... is ... low ... enough, Flea." Li'l Jack spoke slowly, as if to a mentally deficient person. "Blast it all! Ye're becoming a blithering blighter. Dismissed." Making little waving motions with his claw, he turned away, seeming to forget them completely.

"Come along, li'l miss," Flea said. Grabbing the rope binding her hands together, he pulled. Piper stumbled after him in a daze.

"Where the heck is she?" Zonk asked.

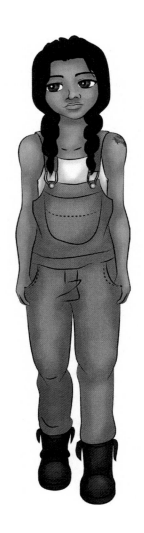

CHAPTER SIXTEEN

Gone

Zonk woke first. She lay in her hammock, suspended in the Underground Home. She stretched, and peered around. All the other girls still slept—Pudge and Midge in their respective hammocks, and Stinky, the twins, and Thumb in the big bed that used to belong to the Lost Boys. How could this be, she wondered? She never woke first. She rubbed her eyes. It must be something about the Neverland. She was too excited to sleep.

Wriggling out of her hollow tree exit, dusty-yellow light met her eyes. The sun was well up. How come Pipsqueak—that is Piper Pan, she really was going to try to call her Pan—hadn't awakened them? "Rowing at sunrise." That's what she'd said last night.

Shielding her eyes from the pale glare of the sun, Zonk peered up into the tree. They'd all worked hard yesterday and played hard last night. Maybe Pipsqueak—*Pan*, had overslept too. She braced her hands on the lowest limb and swung her feet up. Waking up Pan ought to be fun.

Pan. I mean, how cool is that? Zonk searched for the

next handhold. Sure, she was a little envious—who wouldn't want to find out they were Peter Pan's heir? But mostly she was just plain happy for Pipsqueak. The kid seemed like she deserved a break. Fitch hadn't liked her, and that usually meant a person was worth knowing.

Plus, she and the other girls wouldn't be here if it weren't for Piper. They were all happy as clams to be free, even if this place was a total wasteland and, according to Pip, cursed with a people-eating dragon. The kid wanted them to be "Pan's Merry Band." Well, that might not be so bad. The hard part was getting them all to agree on anything! Zonk grinned as she climbed higher and higher.

Wait. She stopped climbing. *Where was Pan's hammock?* She stepped from one limb to another, all the way around the tree. Something was wrong. The hammock had hung about ten feet in the air, and she stood at least fifteen feet off the ground right now. The velour sword-bag hung just above her, but the hammock was nowhere in sight.

She shook her head. Maybe Piper was playing a joke on them. But that didn't seem right. The kid had been working them all to the bone. She wasn't the joking type. This must be some other kind of test.

Climbing back down, Zonk's mind raced. Maybe

they could play their own joke on Piper. She hurried back down into the Underground Home, whistling cheerfully. She jostled one girl, then the next, until they were all awake. "Piper's playing a trick on us. Let's go pretend we went rowing without her."

Pudge shrugged, rubbing her sleepy eyes. "Fine by me. I hate those drills. It'll give us an excuse to eat breakfast right away instead of later."

They all piled outside, panting as they lay on the ground in mock exhaustion. Midge and Pudge went for honey and spring water. The others talked loudly about how well rowing practice had gone.

Half an hour later, they were all starting to get concerned.

"Where the heck is she?" Zonk asked.

Thumb removed the dandelion stem she was chewing. "I dunno."

"Where'd you get that flower?" Flim asked, continuing the complicated hand-clapping pattern she was doing with her twin.

"Found it hewe by the twee this mowning," Thumb replied.

"Does it taste better than your thumb?" Flam said.

"Uh-huh," Thumb replied, nodding solemnly.

"What about Belle? Has anyone seen her?" Stinky peered around hopefully.

"Give it a break, Stinky." Pudge elbowed the younger girl.

"Hey, why can't you call me Sara?" Stinky objected. "I've only farted once since we got here."

"It's probably our new diet," Midge said.

"Or from starvation," Pudge moaned. "Stinky's your name. I don't care if you fart or not."

They all sat in silence, listening to the quiet, hoping it would be broken.

When lunchtime rolled around, they were really worried. They'd walked the whole area in widening circles, past Kidd's Creek to the mouth of Crocodile Creek and the small bay where the dugout canoe was stowed, and in the opposite direction to the source of Mysterious River, where they were now.

"Mystewious Wivew's whewe Belle lives," Thumb said from her piggyback seat on Zonk.

Everyone stared at her.

"How do you know that?" Zonk asked. You never knew with Thumb. She was quiet for ages and you forgot she was there, then she'd say something and you'd realize she had big ears for a little pitcher. Plus, she never forgot anything she heard.

Thumb shrugged. "She said so."

No one else had heard it, but if Thumb said she'd heard it, she had. They looked at each other, all thinking the same thing.

"Let's find Belle's place," Midge said. "If she's not at home either, we've got real trouble." Midge looked around the circle. Pudge looked like she was going to object, but then shrugged.

Zonk nodded her vote, and they set off.

They stumbled along to the north, as Thumb suggested, for what must have been at least an hour, through brown and gray landscape.

"It's like a black and white movie here," Flim said.

"*Sí*," Flam agreed. "Too bad we cannot save it."

"It would be way too much work," Midge said. "We'd have to spend years planting seeds and waiting for them to grow. Never mind figuring out how to water them!"

"Belle said Pan can save the Neverland," Stinky insisted.

"That was before she found out Pan couldn't fly," Pudge said.

"Or laugh," Flam added.

"Or crow," said Flim.

"Besides, I think Belle is totally wrong about Pipsqueak," Pudge said. "Does she really seem like 'Piper Pan' to you?"

"If Belle says she is, then she is." Stinky's lower lip jutted out.

"I would never waste my time waiting around for the impossible," Pudge jeered.

"One thing's for sure," Midge said loudly, nipping the argument in the bud. "This place would need a miracle to make it green again."

Stinky gasped. "Look!"

Zonk looked where Stinky pointed. A burnished stump, complete with windows, doorways, turrets, and balconies, stood on the far bank of the river, nestled in green moss. Patches of crocus and jonquils encircled it, dotted with grape hyacinth and clumps of lily of the valley. Trailing vinca clung to the riverbank, blooming wildly. Its purple blossoms buzzed with bees.

"Wow." Zonk said. "First flowers I've seen here." She shifted Thumb, riding piggyback.

"Except fow my dandelion this mowning," Thumb said.

"Yeah," Pudge sighed, "it's like magic. Let's go look."

They waded across the still narrow, shallow river and climbed the opposite bank. Taking care not to crush any flowers, they took turns peeking into what was clearly a fairy castle.

"It's beautiful," Stinky breathed.

Zonk pointed. "No staircases."

"That makes sense," Pudge said. "Who needs stairs when you can fly?"

"Well, Belle isn't home." Midge folded her arms

and frowned. "That's clear." No one could argue. The fairy was nowhere to be seen.

"Now what?" Thumb asked.

Flim and Flam looked at each other. "Let's go back to camp," they said in unison. "*Vámonos.*"

They found camp as empty as they'd left it. Clustering around the campfire remains with the others as if to somehow draw comfort from it, Zonk looked at the other girls' faces. Bravado was long gone. Expressions of worry and helplessness had taken hold.

Stinky started to cry. Thumb followed suit.

"Aw, cut it out, guys," Pudge said. "You're making me feel bad here. We're supposed to be Pan's Merry Band, right? You don't look merry at all with tears running down your cheeks."

Zonk raised an eyebrow. Pudge never would have said that if Piper were here.

It was supposed to be funny, but it only made Stinky cry harder.

"They've left us h-here all alo-one," the blonde girl wailed.

Zonk patted the frightened girl gently on the back. "Nah. They wouldn't." Her earlier thought returned to her. "What if it's a test?"

They met her eyes uncertainly.

"Like a trial. To be the Merry Band, we have to pass."

Thumb had her old friend planted firmly in her mouth, but she stopped crying.

"Wh-what do you mean?" Stinky snuffled.

"*Buena idéa*," Flim said. "Good idea," Flam chimed in. They both looked at Zonk.

"So what do we have to do to pass?" Flam asked.

"It might or might not be a test." Midge's voice came from the base of the Never Tree. She stood peering into the branches overhead. "But I do think Pipsqueak—I mean Pan—needs our help." She pointed up. "C'm'ere, guys."

They clumped around Midge.

"See there? That's where the hammock was."

"How do you know?" Stinky asked, drying her eyes.

"Look carefully. See the clumps of torn spider web?" Midge pointed. Eyes followed. "It's sloppily torn. There're a few long pieces still hanging." Nods of agreement met her words. "I think if Pan was playing a practical joke, she'd have done a neater job."

"You mean if she wanted us to believe her hammock had disappeared into thin air, she wouldn't have left a trace?" Pudge laughed. "You're really something, Midge."

Midge looked stern. She eyed Pudge, checking for an insult.

"*Carambas*," Flam exclaimed.

"Oh my gosh, you're right," Flim echoed her twin's sentiments.

Zonk squinted, examining Midge's evidence. She slowly nodded her agreement.

"So ... What do you think really happened?" Pudge asked the question hanging in everyone's minds.

Midge eyed them all in silence, her expression sober. "I think she was captured."

"Capshuwed? What's 'at mean?" Thumb asked.

"It means taken prisoner," Pudge said. "By who?"

"By whom." Midge corrected.

"Ah, shut up," Pudge elbowed Midge in the ribs. "Who do ya think did it?"

"The pirates," Zonk said.

"Pirates?" Flim and Flam looked at each other and started a mock swordfight between them. "Argh! Take that, matey!"

"Cut it out." Pudge stilled them with a look. Her eyes sought the mountains to the south. "That's the direction Piper said the pirate ship is anchored, right?"

"Mmm-hmm," Zonk said. "Who's the pirate captain again?"

"Captain Li'l Jack," Midge growled, her voice a perfect copy of Pan's when she'd imitated the villain for them all.

They laughed. Smiles wreathed faces. Zonk's spirits rose.

"So what do we do?" Pudge asked. "Don't tell me we're going to try to save her. Those are real pirates! We're just a bunch of loser girls!"

"Says you," Zonk growled.

"Maybe we should ask Belle to take us back to Seattle," Stinky said.

The objections to that idea made Zonk happy. She kept a straight face though, and said, "Let's just take a nap and pretend this hasn't happened." She couldn't keep from smiling when everyone glared at her. "Just kidding!" she reassured them.

"She needs us," Thumb said, simply.

"We can fight!" Flim said.

"*Sí, por supuesto,*" Flam agreed.

"Sure we can," echoed Flim.

"If we're going to help, we'll have to work together," Zonk cautioned. It seemed like long odds. "And we'll need a plan."

As one, they all turned to Midge. Zonk figured now would be a good time for the know-it-all to strut her stuff. She always talked like she knew best, but truly taking the lead would be new for her. Besides, Zonk thought, if she falls on her face, there's always Pudge. Pudge would lead them all right, there just wouldn't be a plan.

"Well," Midge said, "I've been thinking about that. There are four things in our favor. One: the pirates must not know we're here, or they'd have taken us too."

Thumb gasped.

"It's okay," Zonk reassured her.

"Two: we know a lot about the pirates, and about Peter Pan and the things he did to get the best of them. Remember watching the movie over and over at Fitch's?"

The girls nodded.

"We can take a tip from the movie. That's number three: pirates are terribly superstitious."

"What's 'at mean?" Thumb mumbled around her thumb.

"You really shouldn't suck your thumb, you know," Midge said. "You'll get buck-teeth."

"Leave off," Zonk snapped. Lowering her mouth to Midge's ear, she spoke more gently. "Not now."

Midge nodded at Zonk and swallowed. "Superstitious means they believe in ghosts," she explained.

"So we're gonna be ghosts?" Flim and Flam wiggled their fingers at each other. "Ooooooooooh!" They wailed.

"If you two don't cut it out, I'm gonna separate you," Pudge threatened.

Midge cleared her throat. "Do you, or do you not want to hear my plan?" She waited until quiet reigned. "Most important of all is number four: *we fight like girls*." She leaned forward and began to outline her plan.

CHAPTER SEVENTEEN

High Tide

It was late afternoon by the time the Merry Band piled into the dugout and began paddling down Kidd's Creek.

"Stwoke, stwoke," Thumb called the rhythm from her seat in the bow.

Zonk glanced at the sky, calculating the position of the dimming sun. They only had about two hours of daylight left. She had no idea what awaited them in Kidd's Cove, or if they'd even find Pan alive. Not wanting to frighten the others, she hadn't shared her visions of Piper's quick death by firing squad. But when she exchanged glances with Pudge, seated next to her, she knew she wasn't the only one imagining such dark things.

Zonk showed Pudge how to do a "C" stroke and a "J" stroke. Together in the stern, they used the strokes to manage the steering. Not that the floating boat needed much help following this slow, old creek to the sea. Midge and Stinky shared the bow bench closest to Thumb, and Flim and Flam threw their weight into powering the boat from the middle.

They'd stowed Pan's rudder paddle in the boat, hoping beyond hope for a trip home including all eight of them. Their friend's backpack, including her change of clothes, also lay in the boat's hull, as did the velour-wrapped swords. Fortunately, Pan's captors had missed the weapons. The mast and "no-pirate" flag stayed stowed as well, for the time being.

It had taken time to launch their rescue. They'd had to hike overland to retrieve the boat from its sheltered cove. Normally the dugout would have been far too heavy for them to carry, even with seven pairs of hands. Six, actually. Thumb wasn't tall enough to reach, though she insisted on joining them. Fashioned from a hollowed-out log as it was, the boat seemed to weigh a ton.

Luckily, the dose of pixie dust Belle had given it the night of their escape hadn't completely worn off. The boat no longer flew, but it felt feather-light as they portaged back to Kidd's Creek. The oars and mast were buoyant enough that Thumb could carry them in an over-the-shoulder sling they made out of Pan's pink no-pirate flag.

Once gathered at Kidd's Creek, Midge made them all roll on the muddy banks. "Camouflage," she said. "I don't want to see light colors left on any of you. Especially you white girls." She glared at Pudge and Stinky. "Don't forget your faces and hands."

Everyone groaned at that, but rolling in the mud hadn't been half bad.

Filthy and anxious to be off, they'd clambered aboard. Zonk had Thumb set a quick paddling pace in an effort to offset the sluggish current.

By the time Zonk heard the lap of ocean waves over the quiet trickle of their creek, the sun was preparing to hide its face for the night. Its color, as it got ready to go down, was the most intense they'd seen here yet. Instead of graying yellows highlighting the clouds, reds and pinks burned across the sky.

"Ohhhh," Stinky said, her voice reverent.

"It's like the Wizard of Oz movie," Flam said.

Flim wiggled in her seat, excited. "When Dorothy arrives in Oz! *Colores!*"

"It's beautiful," Pudge said, her voice hushed.

"It gives me the willies," Zonk whispered back. "Help me get us to the bank over there," she gestured with her paddle. Raising her voice just a tad, she said "Give me some power, everyone. Midge and Stinky: be ready to climb out and pull the boat up."

Once ashore, they stowed the boat in the brush atop the creek bank.

"Put the paddles and our other stuff over there," Midge directed in a whisper. She pointed to a lone birch tree. "It'll be our marker so we can find it again."

None of them knew how close the pirates might be. They spoke in whispers and tiptoed, hoping it would help them stay hidden. If they lost the element of surprise, they were sunk.

"All right," Midge said. "We need to figure out the lay of the land, and fast, before the sun sets completely. We'll travel low to the ground, and single file. Spread out some. That way if one of us is seen, the others may still have a chance. I'll lead the way." She stopped, looked at the ground, and scratched her head. "Or maybe—"

"Midge!" the girls chorused.

Answering Midge's panicked glance, Zonk nodded in reassurance. "It's a good plan."

Midge gulped and blinked. "OK. Pudge, you come behind me. Zonk, I want you bringing up the rear for now. Keep an eye on the little ones."

"Little ones!" Flam protested.

"Who's little, *Shorty*?" Flim growled.

Midge just shook her head and moved off toward the rise in a half-crouch.

Everyone else followed suit, twigs snapping at every step.

Zonk winced. Obviously, they weren't yet capable of moving silently through the brush. She hoped the pirates were busy doing loud pirate things, whatever that meant.

Ahead, Midge neared the top of the rise. She gestured with one arm for them to get down and come close.

Sprawling on her belly, shoulder to shoulder with the others, Zonk peered over the ridge at what lay below. From here, the ground dropped steeply to a beach of white sand. Water lapped at the shore. Dark waves reflected bits of the sunset's color, like shattered stained glass.

Down the beach to their right, the flames of a bonfire mirrored the blood red of sky and water. Figures moved in the dusky light, voices rose in a whiskey-pitched tune. The pirates. A hundred feet out from shore hulked the dark form of an anchored vessel. The *Jolly Roger*.

"Wow. That's some ship," Zonk murmured in admiration.

"Look there." Midge whispered, pointing to a spot midway between the windjammer and the blaze on the beach. "The third piling out."

Zonk squinted in the indicated direction and froze. She'd seen the line of old pilings—the remains of a long-gone dock. But she hadn't noticed the figure lashed to one of the pilings until Midge pointed it out. She should have. Grubby as it might be, the sweatshirt-clad figure tied to the pier couldn't be anyone but Piper.

Pan. She stood proudly, dark hair blending in with the waterlogged piling behind her. Her hands were bound in front, pinned by ropes at her waist. More rope cinched her chest and knees to the pier as well. The sun's final rosy rays showed her angular pale face, features set in determined stoicism. She wasn't gagged, but she uttered not a sound. She stood still, a proud statue to the casual eye.

Her hands grasped each other tightly, and a receding wave exposed bare toes clutching the sand in a death-grip. Ropes stretched sideways from her ankles, weighed down with a series of large rocks. Another wave curled, encircling Pan's knees. Her jeans were wet to the thighs.

The tide was coming in. One glance at the beach showed Zonk the high tide line. High tide would leave Pan underwater.

Belly clutching in fear, Zonk turned to the others. She nodded to Midge. "Talk fast."

Midge gulped, her eyes uncertain. She drew a deep breath. "Okay. I'm still not sure this is the best plan, but you all remember what we talked about. Zonk, I'm with you. We'll use the dugout. Pudge, you take the others. Three rooster crows means 'meet back here.' Thumb, don't you give the signal. It'll sound like an owl."

Flim snorted. "Yeah, "Woo, woo, woo, woo, woo!" She parodied an "r-less" crow.

Nervous laughter hissed, like air leaking from a bicycle tire. Thumb stuck out her tongue.

Midge reached her clutched fist out to the cluster's center. "Good luck." Six other hands piled on. "Everybody?"

They looked at each other, hope and fear warring in their eyes. They were about to attempt to do something together, something really important. That was new, and it felt good.

Hands pumped together three times in rhythm. "Pan's Merry Band!" They broke, each girl focused on what she had to do.

Zonk drew Midge to her side, and they watched the other mud-covered girls disappear into the woods.

🗡

Enthroned by the red armchair his men had carried ashore for him, Captain Li'l Jack beamed. Seated just so, he could enjoy the warmth of the fire without it eclipsing his view of the coming execution.

He didn't often condone drunken carousing among his crew, but tonight offered the perfect occasion. All hands save one, manning the *Jolly Roger*'s crow's nest, were here on the beach. He'd ordered enough whiskey brought from the ship for all.

Deep in their cups, the men were doing a jig 'round the fire and singing old seafaring tunes. They'd come ashore a few hours ago to roast the pig he'd snagged from a butcher on his last raid. The captain avoided the whiskey; he didn't want his wits dulled. Rather, he sat sipping fizzy water, relishing the sight of Pan's silly heir strapped to the piling.

She'd been there since morning, all through the tide going out. At low tide, the beach had been a wonderfully smelly place. The scrawny girl had stood in slimy green seaweed, sand fleas jumping about her legs.

"Flea, there were plenty of barnacles on that piling, weren't there?" he crooned to his First Mate.

"Aye, Cap'n. Covered in barnacles, it was."

"Excellent," he said. "Pity I can't see her back from here." He warmed to the image: razor-sharp shells slicing the girl's back, stripes of blood seeping into her shirt.

He loved a good bloodthirsty scene. He'd almost succumbed earlier to the temptation to lynch a crewmember or two. He could always spare at least one in the interest of feeding his blood lust.

The tide had turned mid-afternoon. He'd

passed the girl when they rowed him ashore for the celebration. "The dratted thing is keeping up a brave front," he snarled at his First Mate. "She'll scream before the end," he promised himself. "The water is fairly warm, is it not, Flea?"

"Oh, aye, Cap'n. As a li'l un's bath."

"Good," he snapped, adding "I'd hate to have her die prematurely of hypothermia." Oh no. He wanted to watch her terror as the water rose, higher and higher, finally covering her mouth, then her nose. Her eyes would still show when she drowned, and he'd have the pleasure of watching them.

He wished the tide would hurry. He didn't want it to grow too dark to see.

A memory stole across his mind. He was a small boy newly arrived from England, fresh on the *Jolly Roger*, squeamish at the sight of blood. Afraid of pain, terrified by death, it had taken years of training to become merciless.

He'd succeeded. He'd disciplined his mind and nerves, steeled them to the task of gaining the world's respect. He'd crushed the tendrils of empathy, squeezed the life from the buds of mercy, torn out those weeds that threatened the fertile black soil of his heart.

It took only one image to keep him on track. A sight he'd witnessed, long ago. He let the vision play: his father and mother, sitting on their bed. A new baby brother lay cradled in his mother's lap. His father's arm wrapped about his mother's shoulders.

"*This* is our son, Harriet," his father said. "We spend our attention on *him*. This baby boy, Charles, will grow to be a fine and respected man. Capable and strong and handsome."

"Yes, Tom." His mother rested her head on his father's shoulder. His baby brother's tiny fingers curled around her graceful forefingers.

Eight fingers and two thumbs. Jack could see them from where he stood, hidden behind the doorjamb.

His mother sighed. "I only wish I'd never taken that medicine. If I'd just borne the morning sickness without it, our John might be whole."

"Never mind that now." His father played with the baby's toes with his free hand and kissed his mother's hair. "No use crying over spilt milk, and all that."

Next came the words that drove Jack into the English night where he eventually found his way to Tink and the Neverland.

"We concentrate on Charlie now, love," his father said. "John will never amount to anything. He's a cripple. He'll be no good to anyone, not even himself. Even without those horrid flippers."

With difficulty, Captain Li'l Jack brought his focus back to the present. Back to the scene before him on the beach. He shoved away the vexing thought flickering at the edges of his mind: that child bound to the pier out there might, once, have been himself.

†

With Zonk's help, Midge arrived at the *Jolly Roger*'s hull, having traveled under cover of the dugout canoe. Upside-down, it appeared to be a floating log—completely innocent. Remains of pixie-dust kept the hollowed inside floating higher than usual. Each girl held onto a bench, easily keeping her head above water in the air trapped inside. Midge thought this was great, as she was a timid swimmer.

In anticipation of their return, the pirates had left a rope ladder dangling over the ship's side. Midge's teeth clenched with nerves as she gripped the rope. She pushed herself away from the dugout.

"Reach up a little farther," Zonk coaxed. "That's it. Now walk your feet up the ship's boards. A little higher—you've got it. Get both feet on the rope rung—good. Now start climbing."

Zonk's voice was just above a whisper—although Midge was pretty sure no one would hear them over the bawdy singing coming from the beach. Sweat beaded on Midge's forehead and upper lip. The cool evening breeze off the water should be making her cold. Fear goes a long way to warm a body at a time like this, she thought wryly.

From the top of the ladder, Midge looked back down at Zonk, sent a thumbs-up sign, and waved her on. She watched as Zonk ducked back under the inverted dugout, maneuvered it to the *Jolly Roger*'s bow, then disappeared from sight. Midge crossed her fingers, praying that Zonk would make it to Piper before it was too late.

While Zonk wore one of Pan's daggers at her belt to cut Piper free, Midge carried one of the twins' slingshots. Flim and Flam had made a pile—they still had plenty. Midge knew she'd be useless with one of Piper's swords, and the daggers, while less clumsy, made her nervous. If she carried a dagger, she might have to use it. Somehow, the slingshot seemed more benign.

Well, no more putting it off. Taking a deep breath, Midge prepared to carry out her mission.

†

Piper shivered. The water surging around her waist wasn't so very cold, but hunger and thirst made her tremble. Try as she might to fool herself, she was afraid. Death by drowning. A horrible thought, made worse by the moment as the water rose.

To distract herself, she'd spent the day concentrating on watching things. Really *looking*, trying to memorize details. She told herself stories about seaweed, about sand fleas, about the sea. She avoided the pirates, both with her eyes and in her stories. They just reminded her of her plight.

At the moment, her eyes followed the progress of a log drifting toward her. She'd first seen it floating off the point of the cove. It drifted across the inlet, which was odd. That wasn't quite the direction of the current. It disappeared behind the *Jolly Roger*.

It ought to have stayed snagged behind the ship with the tide's pressure. She'd been surprised to see it emerge on the other side. Now it drifted toward shore. She stood directly in its pathway.

"Great," she muttered. "My head will be crushed between it and the piling." Well, a blow to the head is probably better than drowning, she thought miserably.

Darkness pressed closer around her. In spite of her intentions, she glanced toward the beach. The dancing light of the fire illuminated the pirates' wild antics. The chair where Captain Li'l Jack sat lurked at one side of the fire. She could see his form, but not his face.

"Come here, ye slimy sack of entrails." The captain's voice carried easily over the water. Pirates stopped their merry-making. Several looked both ways and pointed to their own chests, each hoping the captain meant someone else. "Yes, you, ye parasitic swab. The one with the eye patch. How d' ye lose that eye, sailor?"

"Uh, Cap'n, meaning no harm Cap'n," the man stammered. "Ye poked it out with yer hook in a blind rage."

"Blind rage, eh? I hope I kept the 'rage' since I gave you the 'blind.'"

The crew laughed. It had a forced sound to it.

It was probably laugh or be killed, Piper thought.

"Step over here before I loose my rage on yer other eye." The captain's quiet threat sent a shudder through Piper.

The pirate crept toward the captain, head bowed, like a naughty child caught at school.

"Quit sulking and make a bloody torch, man. A long one. Then carry it out to the piling and sink it into the sand. Or tie it to the piling itself, I don't care which. Just don't make me miss the sublime sight of Pan's last moments."

Piper closed her eyes in despair. She'd been grateful to at least have the coming darkness veil her from the captain's gaze. The water lapped at her armpits. Soon it would reach her shoulders and her neck. She'd have to die in the spotlight. The evil man was denying her single remaining mercy: to leave the world while cloaked in night's privacy.

CHAPTER EIGHTEEN

Uninvited Guests

Midge focused on her mission: set the *Jolly Roger* on fire, get the heck off of it, and swim back to the rendezvous point.

Peering over the ship rail, she looked around carefully. Probably at least one pirate was still on the ship, keeping a lookout. At least with her black hair and her usual all-black clothes, Midge was set for night camouflage. She'd reapplied mud to her skin before she and Zonk had set off.

All quiet onboard—so far. Midge swung one leg over the ship's rail, then the other, dropping on deck with her bare feet. Oh, shoot, Midge thought, I forgot my feet. The water had washed them clean, and now they seemed to glow in the twilight. She tiptoed quickly toward the amidship hatch. Just as she began descending the ladder, she heard a whistle and froze.

It came from above. Looking up through masts, stowed sails, and rigging, she could just see the lookout. It took about six notes for Midge to realize he was whistling "Ring Around the Rosy," not whistling at her. Still, she had no idea if the tune might be a code to warn fellow pirates against an intruder. If she could see him, that meant he could have seen her as well. Stomach in her throat, she moved faster down the ladder.

She needed to find the captain's quarters. That couldn't be too hard. Arriving below deck, she turned, propelling herself forward. The captain's cabin would likely be at the back of the boat. A creaking noise stopped her in her tracks, and something brushed her face. A scream rose from her chest.

Clapping a hand over her mouth to stop the sound, she inhaled deeply through her nose, trying to calm her pounding heart. It was horribly dark down here. What she wouldn't give for a flashlight about now!

Eyes adjusting to the dimness, she saw that her attacker was a hammock. She nearly giggled with relief. Hammock after hammock hung, only about a foot and a half apart, across the entire ship's width. Ropes creaked lightly against supporting wooden beams, as the ship rocked on light waves. Now that she knew what the sound was, Midge reeled in her fleeing courage. She hoped all the hammocks were empty. She wasn't about to check, that was for sure. She reached, with difficulty, into her pants pocket, extracting one of the pebbles she carried as slingshot ammunition.

Light glowed faintly through a narrow doorway ahead, down a very dark hallway. She tiptoed toward the light, hands stretched in front of her. It seemed to take forever, but the glow brightened as she went. It became a shaft of lantern light striping the flooring, pouring from a door hanging slightly ajar. Midge stood flattened against the adjacent wall. She leaned very slowly to the side, until one eye peeked inside.

†

Having given the order to light Pan's death scene, Captain Li'l Jack waited impatiently. The one-eyed pirate took forever tying his shirt in a wad to the end of a branch and dousing it in kerosene. The man had finally finished, when they heard the noise.

It was a high noise. Long and drawn out, it chilled the captain's bones and made every man near him shudder. It seemed to come from the woods behind the beach.

"What's that?" barked the captain. He forced his voice to be loud and strong when it wanted to wheeze in fright. "Flea! What was that noise?"

"I don't know, Cap'n," his First Mate replied.

"Well, find out, Flea!" The roar came easily this time. Sometimes he wanted to shake that blasted little man until the few teeth he had left in his wild-haired head fell out.

"Aye aye, Cap'n." Flea stumbled over the foot of a pirate lounging next to him and nearly fell face-first into the fire. Only the speed of the one-legged deckhand saved the First Mate. The fellow grabbed his belt and hauled him back to his feet. "Aye aye, sir," Flea squeaked in terror and rushed into the darkness, only to slow as he reached the edge of the dead forest.

It was so dark now, and the fire so bright, the captain could barely make out the outlines of the tree-trunks. The sound came again. Louder this time, it keened like a mother who'd lost her child.

Flea scuttled back to the captain's side, trembling. "It seems to come from the woods, Cap'n."

"I can hear that, you fool! Send a scurvy sailor to find the cause, or ye'll go yerself."

Knobby knees quaking, Flea spun around three times, one hand over his eyes, the other outstretched. When he came to a stop, his arm pointed to the one-legged fellow who'd saved him. "Sorry, mate," Flea mumbled.

The chosen man clumped toward the woods, sword drawn, and disappeared into the darkness.

Moments later, screams of shock and terror lanced the night. They went on rather a long time, those screams of agony, before silence fell.

Captain Li'l Jack waited, squinting into the darkness, willing the sailor to reappear. Seconds stretched into minutes, seeming like an eternity. Then, horror of horrors, the wail sounded again. High and elongated, it brought visions of a wounded woman to mind.

"What ghost is this?" the captain whispered, for his ears alone. "Which of me victims would choose this moment to haunt me?"

Claw reaching to his belt, he clasped the butt of his gun, raised it to shoulder level, and positioned his hook to pull the trigger.

Pirates around him, seeing what was coming, flattened themselves on the sand.

He fired. Blessed silence followed.

The ghost cried again. This time it seemed as though there were two, wailing in harmony.

†

The ghostly wails sent shivers down Piper's spine. She had a horrible feeling she'd heard those voices before. A vivid image bloomed in her mind, which she tried in vain to banish, of the Lifers caught out there in the captain's deadly web.

Just a foot away from Piper's face, the floating log threatening to crush her head stopped its forward motion. Piper stared at the water around her. Had the tide already turned? Maybe the pirate had miscalculated and high tide wouldn't be high enough to drown her. She felt a wave of hysteria rise, and giggled. It would serve the conniving toad right. But the water was lapping the underside of her chin now. It didn't need to rise much farther. Still, the log held its place, a foot away.

Then it moved sideways, two feet to the right, and came toward her again, this time alongside, floating under the pier. Piper's brows shot up. This was no ordinary log. She sensed something, or someone, behind her. She tensed, ready for anything. Who knew what antics the pirates were up to now?

"Quiet, Piper. It's me, Zonk." A voice, low and sweet, spoke in her ear. "Hold still, I'm going to cut the ropes."

Shock sent Piper's heart skittering. Zonk was here. That meant the rest of the girls were nearby, because Zonk wouldn't have come alone. She was torn between relief and terror. Facing death on her own had been bad, but the possibility that the others might face it as well was much worse. If she lived,

Piper thought—if they all lived—she would forget this crazy idea of revenge. Never mind trying to defeat Captain Li'l Jack. It was far more important to get them all to safety. They needed to get the heck out of the Neverland. Surely her parents would forgive her for that.

†

"You." The captain pointed his claw at the man to his right. Most all of the men stood to his right now, come to think of it. The cowardly lot had moved, putting the bonfire between them and the woods. "Go find that bird, kill it, and bring it to me," he ordered.

The blackguard shook his head like a wet dog. "No, Cap'n. No, Sir. I'll do anythin' for ye but that."

"Cast off, ye cowardly scum, or I'll tear ye from stem to stern with this." His hook glinted in the firelight.

Defeated, the sailor reloaded his pistol and plodded toward the forest, a man marching to his doom.

The poor sod screamed once. No more.

"Blast it all! No ghost is going to get the best of me," the captain seethed. "You." He randomly chose another crewman. "Whatever yer name is. Go kill it."

"Ye can't kill ghosts, Cap'n," the swarthy man squeaked like a girl.

"Ye can *catch* 'em," bellowed Li'l Jack. The fellow ran toward the water, but the captain was faster. Reaching out his hook, he snagged the man's ear.

"Aaayeeee!" The man's scream made some worthless scum wet himself, the captain could smell it. "I said, go catch it," he growled, "and that's what ye'll do." He tore out his hook, smiling at the sound of ripping cartilage.

Clutching his bleeding ear with one hand and his dagger with the other, the man cried all the way to the woods. A moment later his weeping rose to a shriek, becoming at last a "Noooooooo!" trailing into nothing.

"Confound it! Fire! Everyone fire!" Dropping his pistol, Li'l Jack clapped steel and flesh forearms to his ears.

The sound of twenty pistols firing nearly deafened him all the same.

Bingo, Midge thought. This had to be the captain's quarters, judging from the spaciousness and the rich furnishings. She listened carefully. Hearing nothing, she pushed the door farther open, inch by inch, in tandem with the ship's rolling motion. The hinges squeaked. She winced. Nothing for it, she had to get in. When the opening was wide enough, she slipped inside, slingshot loaded and at the ready.

The light came from a lantern, hung from a hook attached to the wall. Was the hook one of the captain's? The hair on the back of her neck stood up, and she reached for the lantern to dispel the shudder rippling down her spine. Lantern in hand, she inspected the cabin. She was looking for anything useful that might be used as ransom, if necessary, to free Pan. There might be valuables, or even better, incriminating information. Blackmail would be a more powerful tool against this pirate captain than paying him with his own treasure.

The first thing that caught her eye was a table sparkling with china, crystal, and silver. Food still stood on several of the serving platters. Her stomach growled. She hadn't eaten solid food since she'd arrived. She wasn't hungry, but the succulent smells made her mouth water. She nabbed a piece of ham and, while chewing, raised the lantern to see what other treats she could help herself to.

The boom of many guns going off at once

nearly gave her a heart attack. She swung around, feeling the blood drain from her head.

CHAPTER NINETEEN

From the Fat into the Fire

Piper felt Zonk's hand holding her still as she sawed loose the ropes binding her—first her wrists, then her waist, one leg, then the other. Rope by rope, Piper's bonds fell away. Piper stood, shaking, until Zonk came up for air behind her again.

"Zonk. You shouldn't have come," she whispered.

"Why not?" Zonk asked. Her voice was soothing. "You don't begrudge us our own adventure in the Neverland, do you?"

"No, but—if anything happens to any of you, I couldn't stand it," Piper said.

"The only thing happening is, you're free," Zonk said, a smile in her voice. "Now, time to swim. See that point on the other side of the cove? That's our rendezvous point." Her voice took on an edge. "Start swimming, *now.*"

"The others?" Piper asked.

"Haven't you heard those ghost calls?"

Recognition sent a shiver down Piper's spine.

Guilt twisted her gut. The others were serving as bait while Zonk freed her. "Oh, no ... "

Zonk gave Piper a push. "Go. Swim. Now."

"What about you?" Piper tried to quiet the shaking of her limbs, the chattering of her teeth. Some removed part of her noted she must be in shock.

"Never mind about me. I have the dugout here."

Piper started. She hadn't recognized the boat. Upside-down in the water, it looked completely different. "Oh. Well, I'll hide under it too," she said. "I'm not leaving you—"

Piper gasped at the sound of twenty pistols firing at once, but the scream that followed ripped through her like a chainsaw.

⸸

Deafened as Captain Li'l Jack was by the cacophony of twenty pistols firing, he couldn't miss the scream. It was a babe, if the shrieking that followed was any measure. Although which of his tiny victim's souls might be crying in his woods this night, he hadn't a clue. The ghostly wails had been bad, this was worse. A child ghost was the worst curse a pirate could call down.

Every pirate took a step back. Then another. And another.

A few more steps and his crew would be running away in terror.

"Don't … move … a … single … muscle." Li'l Jack's jaw ached from clenching it. "Any of ye," he said, "or it'll be yer last."

" … Thumb!" Piper and Zonk spoke the little girl's name at the same time, their bodies jerking automatically toward shore—toward the scream and the sobs.

"No!" Zonk grabbed Piper by the shoulder and yanked her back. "Whatever it is, getting ourselves caught won't help."

Piper's mind raced. Clearly, Thumb had been hurt by something. Maybe a bullet, maybe something else, but that scream was no sham. She knew real agony when she heard it. They would have to assume the worst, and go from there. Thumb might be fatally wounded.

An image played on the edge of Piper's awareness. She lay in her birch bark and spider web hammock, suspended from the Hollow Tree while Belle applied tears to her scrapes and scratches. The abrasions had healed at once.

Piper breathed out a hiss of air. All day she'd used thoughts of Belle's betrayal to fuel her anger—and hence her courage—as she waited to die. She'd heaped all of her pain and rage on the ancient fairy. It was Belle's fault she'd lost her parents. Belle's fault she'd arrived too late in the Neverland, that she hadn't made friends of the other foster girls.

It was certainly Belle's fault the two of them could never work together like a proper person and her fairy. The last thought nearly drowned her in sadness, so she'd scooted on from there. She'd almost had a fairy of her own. Losing that, of all things, was too much to bear.

She'd been glad that she'd never see the fairy again. Better to be drowned by the tide than by the overwhelming pain of being betrayed by your very own fairy. Well—Peter's very own fairy, anyway. And now, it turned out, Cap'n Li'l Jack's very own fairy.

But with Thumb's life in danger, she had to see Belle again. She had to free the fairy from that jeweled cage, and hope against hope the little two-timing wretch wouldn't be too drunk to summon those healing fairy tears. Getting Belle was the only sure way to save Thumb.

"I know a way." Piper set her own hand on Zonk's and squeezed. "Give me the dagger."

Zonk handed her the dagger, hilt first. Piper grabbed hold and slid it into her belt.

"Thumb will be all right." Pip hoped her cracked voice sounded convincing. "Stay here, stay hidden. Stay safe, okay? I'll go get what we need." She took a huge breath of air, dropped under water, and pushed clumsily off the pier. Numb as her legs were, she hoped she could swim underwater far enough.

As Midge swung around, heart thumping from the crack of gunshots, the lantern dragged across the table. Plates and glasses crashed onto the floor. She nearly dropped the lantern right then, to set the ship ablaze. Her hand shook, and she thought she was going to puke, but something shiny drew her gaze, and she swallowed back the bile.

It was a gold and jewel-encrusted hanging thing. She moved closer to inspect it, hands unsteady. Her already charged system got yet another shock when she heard a high, gravelly voice from inside.

"Help me!"

Midge tried to peer inside but could see nothing.

"It's me, Belle," the voice came again. "I'm in here."

The old fairy! What in the heck was she doing there? A quick once-over showed Midge that the golden thing was tied shut at the bottom. She set the lantern down on the nearest surface, a decorative side table, and used both hands trying to untie the knots.

"And who in bloody blazes are you?" A nasal, sinister voice came from behind her. A short, scruffy pirate stood in the doorway. It was the lookout, and he held a pistol.

Without pausing to think, Midge grabbed the lantern, and threw it at the pirate. Praise luck, it hit the pistol, knocking it from his hands before shattering on the floor. Flames leapt up immediately. Kerosene splashed on the man, and he screamed as his sleeve caught fire. He turned and ran.

Midge was right behind him. She couldn't let him warn the pirates onshore. She needed more time, for the fire to truly take hold, and mostly, to keep herself and the rest of the Merry Band safe. The sailor jumped for the ladder. Leaping up, she grabbed a foot, and used all her weight trying to drag him back below.

"Curse ye, yeh black-hearted witch! Leave me be!" The man gave a mighty kick, and Midge fell to the floor. Hands scraped, knees bruised, she clamored to her feet, scrambling up the ladder after the lookout. The moment she hauled herself on deck, she rearmed her slingshot and let fly, just as he reached the rail, hands raised in a megaphone shape to warn the pirates onshore.

She heard a *thunk*, and saw the man's head drop forward. She let out her breath in a whoosh. Had her aim really been that good twice in a row?

Another figure appeared at the rail, this one boarding the boat, now face to face with her head-lolling victim. Arms came around the lookout. Midge struggled with her wet pocket, trying to free another pebble. The figures grappled. Suddenly, her lookout assailant toppled over the rail, pitched by the new arrival. She raised her slingshot to try her luck a third time, just as the man hit the water below with a *splash*.

"Midge! It's me! Are you all right?" The new person spoke.

It was sheer luck she hadn't already sent the pebble flying by the time she figured out to whom the voice belonged.

"Pan?" She ran to the wet figure and flung her arms around her. "You're free! Are you all right? What are you doing here? You were supposed to swim to the rendezvous place, unless ... " Midge's eyes widened. She pulled back and clapped a hand to her mouth. "Oh no. Oh no, oh no, oh no!"

"What?" Piper was shaking her, trying to reach her through her panic.

"Belle is below."

"I know," Piper said, darkly.

"Yes, but—the cabin is on fire," Midge said, and stumbled as Pan pushed her toward the ship's rail.

"Get out of here, Midge. Get to the rendezvous. Do whatever your plan says to do next." Pan pushed her again when she hesitated, then dashed to the aft hatch.

Midge crowed three times, climbed over the ship's side and back down the rope ladder, dropped into the water, and dogpaddled toward the rendezvous shore.

†

On the beach, the pirates backed toward the water, away from the pitiful sobs that came from the woods.

"I said, don't ... move ... a ... single ... muscle." Cap'n Li'l Jack's voice was quiet and definitive. "Before anyone does anything, I want that torch carried out to the piling."

The one-eyed sailor came to life from the sand where he'd dropped at the first ghostly wail, lit his torch and ran into the water. Clearly he felt he'd been given the best assignment. He passed the first piling, the second, neared the third. He lifted the torch. The orange glow pushed back the darkness.

Captain Li'l Jack could see the top of the third piling, but no victim. "Drat it all, forever! I've missed the execution," he yelped. All that waiting, and he'd missed it. He stumbled to the water's edge and shouted commands. "Dive in and untie her, ye bloated sea scum. I want to see Pan's body."

The pirate settled his torch in the sand and waded farther into the water, checking the dagger at his belt. Resting one hand on a bobbing log for balance, he aimed for the piling and dove.

All eyes watched from shore.

The one-eyed fool probably can't see properly, the captain thought. Why else would it be taking him so long to cut one small girl's bonds? Li'l Jack stared, willing Pan's limp body to appear.

The torch wobbled as the waves undercut its footings. Slowly it tipped toward the water. As it fell, the captain and his crew caught one final sight before it fizzled out. The log slipped past the piling, revealing the one-eyed pirate's body floating face-up, his dagger thrust in his breast.

When the thrice-repeated sound of a cock's crow came from the *Jolly Roger*, all eyes turned toward the dark ship. Uneasy muttering rose from his crew. Captain Li'l Jack sniffed. He thought he smelled smoke. Not from the bonfire, but coming in on the tide.

"Fire!" The first voice barely whispered the word, then it rose, repeated, one man to the next.

Flea stumbled toward the captain, feet tripping, knees shaking. "F-f-fire, Cap'n!" The little man saluted. His hair, always wild, stood on end, and his wonky eyes rolled in separate directions. "The *Jolly Roger*'s afire, sir!"

"Well, do something about it, Flea!" the captain roared.

Groups of men ran to the water's edge, then halted. They pushed and shoved, all trying to get into the rowboat at once. "Aye aye, Cap'n!" Flea called. His muffled voice came from the center of the rowboat, now heaped with pirates. If the idiots didn't take care, they would capsize the boat and never reach the ship. The captain knew better than to command them to swim. After the death-by-stabbing of their comrade, none would face the sea spirit's wrath.

Captain Li'l Jack wanted to kill someone, anyone within reach. The sound of a cock, thrice crowed, was the signature sound of a Pan. He, the Scourge of the Seven Seas, had been outwitted by a Pan. And not just any Pan. Worst of all, the Pan who'd slipped through his grasp this night was a mere girl.

Someone would suffer for this, not the least of which would be the girl herself.

✝

Piper thanked her lucky stars she'd been on board the *Jolly Roger* before and knew where she was going. Smoke filled the crew's quarters, crowded with hammocks, and fire licked down the hallway. She pulled her wet sweatshirt up over her mouth, dropped as low to the floor as she could, and made her way on all fours down the hallway as fast as she could go. At least her hair was wet—it might just singe rather than burst into flame.

The fire raged in Cap'n Li'l Jack's quarters. Piper shook with fear. But the thought of Thumb dying drove her forward. Charging through flames to the porthole, she thrust it open, leaned out, and gasped in fresh air. It revived her, but did nothing to dispel the horrible taste and feel of smoke in her throat, eyes, and nose. Heat blasted behind her.

Sucking in another sweet breath of air, Piper held it. She covered her head with the hood of her sweatshirt and dove toward the place she'd last seen Belle. Pulling her dagger, she slashed the tie holding the jeweled cover and grabbed hold. Hot metal seared her hand, and she let go, yelping.

Snatching the first fabric her fingers found, she yanked. The tablecloth from under the cozy remains of Belle and the captain's last supper pulled free, sending the rest of the china, food, goblets, and silverware, flying to the floor. Tablecloth clutched like a hot pad, she snatched at the jeweled cover again. This time it came off. A pitiful figure, tiny, white and feathered, lay on the cage floor.

You'd better not be dead! Piper scooped up Belle and tucked her encircling hand inside her sleeve. It would cut the smoke, and hopefully shield the fairy from flames.

Now, to get out. She wished she could fit through the porthole, but there was no chance of that. Back the way she'd come? There must be a closer ladder leading above deck. Piper charged out the door, ignoring the blisters rising on her bared tummy, and turned left.

She only found the hatch by following the billowing smoke. Up the ladder she went, one-handed, not even feeling her burns. Her lungs wanted to burst. She needed air. Reaching deck, she staggered, her head too light. She fell and rolled, conscious of protecting her hand and its cargo. She smacked into something—and prayed it was the ship's rail, not a mast. Clawing her way up, she found the top. It was the rail. Somehow, she got herself on top of it, and launched herself into the sea.

†

Zonk waited until all the pirates had returned to the *Jolly Roger* before moving. Pan had swum off ages ago. Zonk could only pray she'd accomplished whatever it was she said she'd do to save Thumb. She hoped it didn't have anything to do with the fire and shouts from the ship. It was madness out there, and she couldn't bear to think that after all their work to free her, Pan might once again be a captive on the pirate ship.

Belly-down on the sand behind the overturned dugout canoe, Zonk lay hidden. She'd had to wait a good while. The entire crew insisted on going back to the ship by rowboat, refusing to swim the short distance. All of them were terrified of "The avenging sea spirit."

She shook her head when she heard the name. *Avenging sea spirit.* Zonk shuddered. She hadn't wanted to kill the poor man. But when he dove in search of Pan, she was there instead. Only his amazement at finding someone freely swimming about instead of a drowned prisoner allowed her to steal his dagger and stab him before he did just that to her. She shuddered. She couldn't think about that now.

At last the beach showed empty. The moon's dented face shone dimly between one set of clouds and the next. It provided enough light to see by, now that the bonfire no longer blazed.

The pungent smell of doused charcoal warred with the mouthwatering scent of pork fat. Torn between pinching her nose shut and salivating, Zonk watched the sky. When the clouds veiled the moon, she made her move.

Flipping the boat right side up, she grabbed hold and pulled it up the beach. It came easily, still light from fairy dust. No one aboard the *Jolly Roger* would be watching the shore after the evening's terrifying losses, but she stayed as low as she could all the same. She uttered a prayer of thanks for her dark skin—it had helped her remain undiscovered in the water tonight. It was a plus not to glow in the dark like Pudge.

She thought about going for the rendezvous point. She hadn't heard a sound since Midge's rooster crow. Her knees felt weak, and she tried to keep the awful images of Thumb, wounded, from parading across her mind in a dreadful repeating loop. She wished she could paddle the dugout across the water, but she'd no paddle. She might be spotted, anyway. Too risky.

Maybe some of the girls were close by in the woods. They'd taken three pirates captive, unless Zonk had mistaken the men's bellows and screams. Even if most of the Merry Band had gone to the rendezvous point, someone had to stay here to guard the captives. They couldn't possibly drag three grown men through the woods.

Puckering her lips, Zonk whistled a quiet copy of a rooster's crow. That was as close to a code as she could think of. The wood's stillness answered, broken only by the angry pirate captain's voice from the anchored ship. She shook her head, unsure how to proceed. She didn't want to stumble around in these eerie dead trees all night looking for her mates.

Then a faint whistle sounded in response. It was a "Teeth only" whistle, not a full-fledged "pucker-up-and-blow" one. That had to be Stinky. Zonk smiled in spite of the worry that gnawed in her belly

Leaving the dugout at the edge of the trees, she followed the sound. As she moved through the woods, she stopped now and then to whistle, adjusting her course as needed. After a few minutes of weaving through the trees, she saw a tiny clearing ahead. Zonk moved closer, taking care to tread quietly.

The moonlight revealed three terrified pirates—bound, gagged, and seated in a clump on the forest floor. Stinky stood in front of them. With her feet planted wide, a sword in each hand, she looked like an avenging blonde angel. Maybe Joan of Arc had looked like that, Zonk thought, if she'd been a little bit girlie.

"Nice," Zonk said. She wanted to laugh, the scene looked so outrageous, but she made an effort to keep her voice serious.

"I told them if they moved I'd poke out their eyeballs," Stinky said calmly. "And I still will," she said, threatening them with her swords.

"Where's Pan?" Stinky asked. Zonk noticed, with a remote part of her brain, that Stinky no longer sounded stuffed up. The Neverland must be good for her, too.

"She's fine, as far as I know," Zonk said. "I got to her in time."

"Thumb?" Stinky asked.

Zonk felt the rush of fear return, full force. "I don't know.

"Is she going to die, Zonk?"

Zonk shook her head, trying to look calm when she felt anything but. "Pan said she had a plan."

Piper nearly passed out when she hit the water, having thrown herself from the *Jolly Roger*. The coolness felt good after the fire's blistering heat, but the salt made the blisters on her belly and hands burn. She pulled toward the light, aware of the need to keep Belle from drowning. She emerged, palm first, checking to make sure the little old fairy was still there. She was, crumpled in a heap. Treading water, Piper gently rolled Belle, limp, soggy, and singed, onto her side.

"Don't you dare die on me," she said to the fairy again. Belle had to be all right, for Thumb's sake.

Shouts from the ship made Piper turn her head. Pirates were swarming aboard, running, creating a bucket brigade. Too bad, Pip thought. I wish the whole thing had burned to a crisp. She scissor-kicked through the water, putting more distance between herself and the *Jolly Roger*. The last thing she needed was to be hauled back aboard and condemned to a more immediate means of death.

The fairy in her palm started coughing up water. Convulsing, she hacked and wheezed, finally making it to a kneeling position. Piper felt a rush of relief.

She ignored the mess Belle was making in her hand. Belle was *alive*.

†

A glowing face came toward Zonk and Stinky through the trees.

"Pudge? Is that you?"

"—yeah." Pudge had stopped, doubled over. She gasped and wheezed.

"What is it?" Zonk came to Pudge's side, crouching so she could see the big girl's face in the moonlight. Had the worst happened? Had Thumb died? "Are—are you crying, Pudge?" Zonk peered into Pudge's eyes.

" ... uh ... I don't think so." Another long pause while Pudge drew long, scratchy breaths.

"What happened to Thumb? Was she shot?"

Pudge shook her head. She could still barely talk. "Not shot. Stabbed."

"Stabbed? How? Did one of the pirates get her?" Zonk wanted to shake the answer out of her fellow foster friend. She bit her lip, forcing herself to be patient.

Another shake of the head. "A bullet hit her tree—a branch splintered. Piece of wood flew into her arm. Stabbed her. Bled like a stuck pig."

Zonk felt the blood drain from her head, and her ears rang, like she was going to faint. "Is she dead?"

Pudge winced and shrugged, her expression helpless. "I don't know. I ran right back here to help Stinky."

†

Belle knelt in Piper's palm, held above the waves. Every fairy inch of her ached, throbbed, or burned. She couldn't seem to get her lungs to take in and release air without setting off violent coughing and gagging fits. Surely, she'd swallowed half the inlet by now.

"Glad to see you, too," Belle wheezed, her throat finally cooperating enough to form words.

"I didn't say that, Piper snapped. "I just said 'don't you dare die on me.'"

The girl's eyes were green slits, and Belle could feel the rage sparking from them.

"You betrayed me."

Belle shuddered. The little blood left in her head drained, and she felt faint. A fairy that betrayed her human was lower than low. Even Pearl, the fairy who dealt in black magic, had never stooped to that level. She clutched her middle and coughed, trying to cover her emotion. She hadn't really done that, had she? Somehow she had to regain her composure, try to get the upper hand. "I can explain," she began.

"Oh?" Piper barked the word, and if her eyes had looked daggers at Belle a moment ago, they shot flames at her now. "Don't even try," she snarled.

Belle felt something she hadn't felt for five years: shame. She'd last felt it the night Li'l Jack captured Peter's daughter, Angela, and her husband, Giorgio. The memory seared through her heart and made her throat ache. Belle could have warned them. She might have been able to save Angela and Giorgio. But she'd done nothing. Oh, she'd argued with Li'l Jack over it later, and she'd left for the Crystal City in protest. But she hadn't even *tried* to save Piper's parents. All the blood rushed back to her face with the memory, heating her stinging skin.

"That's better," Piper huffed.

Belle noticed Piper was swimming one-armed, keeping the hand holding her aloft. The girl's breath came short with the effort. Belle felt her accusing stare. Cheeks burning, she refused to meet Piper's eyes.

Piper made a scornful noise. "Now. Listen up. You owe me big time, and you'll start paying your debt tonight."

Belle's throat was raw from coughing. She stared at Piper, wondering what was coming next. She wished she had that glass of after-dinner sherry now—she could use it.

"If there's anything you need to do to generate those healing fairy tears, you'd better start doing it right now," Piper said, teeth gritted to stop them chattering.

Belle could see the girl's gooseflesh and feel her shivers.

"Thumb was hit," Piper said. "Shot, I think."

The look Piper sent her might have been a whip. Belle shuddered.

"I expect you to heal her," Piper continued. "That's the only reason I didn't let you go up in flames along with everything else in that ship's cabin."

Belle sat, still wobbling. She took a deep breath. Lifting her chin, she spoke. "I'll do all I can for Thumb, of course. Completely apart from the debt of my life." She paused a moment, choosing her words. "I won't try to explain my behavior—"

Piper made to snarl at her, but Belle struggled to her feet and held up a hand for silence.

"—we'd only argue over it. But let me say that it was for love of the Neverland."

"Are you sure it wasn't for love of *yourself*, and that pirate?" Piper sneered.

Belle blanched. "Take me to Thumb. What else can I do to repay my debt?"

"I'll let you know," Piper said. "I'll call on you to keep the other girls safe, at any cost, believe me."

"But what about you?" Belle asked. She'd never meant to betray Peter's heir, not really. She'd only been trying to find the fastest way to save the Neverland. The thought of the girl held captive by pirates, facing imminent death, honestly horrified her.

"What about me?" Piper looked startled by sincere concern. "Don't you worry about me," she said, "I'll be fine."

No she wouldn't, Belle thought. She just didn't want anyone getting in the way of her vengeance. She sighed, suddenly exhausted. This child was loyal, and brave. Any fairy would be delighted to have a person like this. Why wasn't she wise enough to be grateful for those qualities?

But Belle couldn't help but feel irritated that the child wouldn't just forget revenge, and learn to fly. There were so many better ways of making her parents' sacrifice worthwhile! Why couldn't Piper seem to see that? Obviously, she'd rather go out in a blaze of glory. The stubborn set of Piper's jaw told Belle she hadn't given up the idea of taking the pirate captain down with her.

Belle was too exhausted to speak her piece. She

would just have to take things a step at a time, and hope she could change Piper's mind along the way.

They had reached the rendezvous promontory. Piper stood in the water, set Belle on her head, and walked to shore.

Belle plunked to a seat, unable to remain standing. She certainly couldn't fly. Grabbing handfuls of Piper's hair to steady herself, she peered into the gloom. Dark figures huddled in a tight group, next to a lone birch tree. Belle felt the lurch in Piper's gait as she stumbled toward them, and understood Piper was every bit as exhausted as she was. When they got close, one of the figures stood, and Belle could see the small figure lying prone in the circle's center.

"This is it, Belle," Piper muttered. "Time to save a life."

She was in an untenable situation. Betrayed by Captain Li'l Jack, she had, in turn, betrayed Piper. Belle straightened her spine. It stopped here. From here on, she would claim the responsibility that was hers. And somehow, she had to make it up to Peter's granddaughter. *If* the child would let her.

CHAPTER TWENTY-ONE

Reunions & Complications

The lump in Piper's throat was so big, she could hardly speak as she joined the girls crouched over Thumb. Midge was there, along with Flim and Flam.

Cradling Thumb's head in her lap, Midge looked up. Worry creased her brow, though she gave Piper a weak smile. "Welcome back," she said.

The twins approached, flanking Piper. Each tucked a hand in her elbow, and leaned against her. They emanated warmth, and something else. Relief? Piper wasn't sure. She just soaked it in like a sponge. She would take any kindness at all, right now. Her body felt bruised, her back was bleeding from barnacle cuts, and she had burn blisters on her belly, her lower back, and her hands. But the absolute worst, was her heart. It felt like it was on the verge of breaking. Thumb might die, and it was all her fault.

"Thumb?" she asked again. Her eyes were used to the dark—she could see Thumb's chest and tummy had been wrapped in—what was that? It must be Pudge's flannel shirt.

"Is she shot?" Piper managed to croak.

"Let me see." Belle's take-charge tone surprised Piper. She'd forgotten the fairy, for a moment, on top of her head for safekeeping. Now Belle dropped to Piper's shoulder, and walked down Piper's right arm. She seemed unable to fly at this point. Piper knelt, holding her hand directly over Thumb's bandage to make getting there as easy as possible.

Belle nodded to Midge. "Go ahead, unwrap the bandage."

"But it's bleeding so much." Midge sounded terrified.

That didn't bode well.

"Bullet?" Belle asked, her voice brisk.

"No. Stabbed by a sharp chunk of wood."

"It'll be all right." Belle stood at Thumb's shoulder, stroking the little girl's hair as she commanded Midge and the twins into action. They loosened the bloodstained bandage.

The dark stain on the shirt over Thumb's skin made Piper gasp. There was so much blood! It centered on her right side, below the shoulder.

Piper became aware that Belle was staring at her. Tears welled in Belle's eyes. The fairy said not a word, but Piper could see the fairy's sorrow, and knew it was the closest she would get to an apology.

Just when the first tear overflowed, Belle turned back to Thumb.

The fairy's tears dropped onto the little girl's wound, and it began to close, like a day lily at night. Sounds of amazement came from Midge and the twins.

"Oh!"

"*Carambas!*"

"*Increíble!*"

"Is there anywhere else?" Belle asked.

Thumb opened her eyes, and pointed to her head.

Belle's tears healed the scrape on Thumb's head as well. "All you have to do is clean up the stained clothes," Belle told the watching girls. "She's all right now."

Piper felt relief pour through her limbs. She hadn't realized how tense she'd been, until this moment.

"Now let me tend *your* wounds." Belle spoke in Piper's ear.

Piper shook her head hard, then slowed, not wanting to knock Belle from her shoulder. "No. I'm fine. It's not important." She didn't know why she said that, when she hurt in so many places from this awful day. It seemed right that she should feel the pain, when it was she who had led these girls into this mess.

"Nonsense. You'll need your strength yet tonight." Belle set about shedding tears on Piper's burns and bruises. She started with Piper's hands, walking rather than flying between them. "Now let me under your shirt."

Piper nodded, unable to take in more than the sight of Thumb's face, gaining in alertness and health. She was vaguely aware of the tickle of Belle's wings on her belly, then her back, and the stinging, burning, aching feelings eased.

She watched Flim and Flam undress Thumb. They washed off the blood and dirt with creek water. When she'd been dried, Piper took the little girl and held her tight. She whispered soft things, gratitude slowly unwinding the knots in her heart. Thumb was all right. Perhaps there was still hope—perhaps they might find a way out of this mess, and back to safety.

Midge pulled dry clothes for Thumb from a bag and handed them to Piper, wordless.

Piper dressed Thumb as gently as she would stroke a butterfly. She didn't want to set her down, this miracle, this one good thing at the end of a horrifying day. Only when Midge had changed did Piper agree to hand Thumb over and change her own sodden clothes.

Only then did she notice the tears pouring down her own cheeks.

✝

Having been convinced to stay put rather than trying to join the others at the rendezvous point, Zonk and Pudge were arguing about what to do with the prisoners.

"Taking them captive was one thing, but I won't be responsible for their deaths," Pudge said.

"What do you care?" Zonk protested. "They'd slit your throat without a second thought!"

"Please, Zonk," Stinky chimed in. "We have to take them somewhere else. The captain and his crew won't come near here for a long time. They'll think it's cursed."

All three turned at the sound of approaching footsteps.

✝

Each step she took toward joining Pudge, Zonk, and Stinky increased Piper's fear. What if they told her to get lost? She'd put them through the ringer. She'd thought of herself as their leader, but what kind of leader got caught before the battle had even begun, not to mention putting the rest of them in mortal danger? She'd hoped the Lifers would be her "Merry Band." But now there'd be no way they'd want that. Sure, Zonk had said they were having their own adventure here in the Neverland, but what if that was just to make her feel better?

"*Ya llegamos!*" said Flam.

"They're just up ahead!" Flim announced, in a whisper pitched for all to hear.

Sure enough, Piper saw the clearing. Pudge, Stinky, and Zonk broke from what looked like an argument, and came toward them.

Zonk turned to see the twins at the edge of the clearing, holding hands. Behind them came Midge, her hands cupped around a tiny glow. Pan brought up the rear, carrying Thumb.

Zonk's heart leapt into her throat at the sight. "Thumb! Is she ... ?" She couldn't finish the question. As Pan handed Thumb to her, Zonk's heart thudded with relief. Thumb's arms encircled Zonk's neck, her legs squeezing her waist.

"I'm all wight," Thumb spoke in Zonk's ear.

The look of sheer terror on Zonk's face solidified

Piper's misgivings. She'd best find a way to slip off and leave the Lifers to themselves.

She had no sooner released Thumb to Zonk's arms, than she was nearly knocked over by Stinky's running hug. "Uff," she grunted. Tentative, she returned the hug. "What's this for?"

"I'm just so glad to see you," Stinky exclaimed.

"You are?" Piper couldn't help asking. She was honestly floored.

"Of course!"

Everyone clustered around, all talking at once.

"Look who got saved from the ship," Midge said, opening her cupped hands to reveal Belle. The aging fairy sat in her "cave" looking somewhat the worse for wear.

Piper couldn't help but notice Zonk's expression, eyes narrowed, as she took in Belle's condition. Well, that was one thing they couldn't blame her for, Piper thought. She hadn't been party to Belle's drinking.

Stinky cooed so much over Belle that Midge finally handed her over.

"She'll be fine," Zonk said, her voice sharp. "She'll have a bad hangover tomorrow, but that's all."

All of a sudden, Piper remembered what Pudge had said about Zonk's mother. That she'd drunk herself to death, wasn't it? Zonk must know what drunk looked like.

Piper still wasn't sure she was welcome here. She shifted, uncomfortable. The other girls continued their chatter.

"It was very fun attacking them," Flim said, elbowing her twin. "Right?"

"*Claro que sí*," her twin agreed. "We pinched, scratched, kicked, pulled hair; we even kneed them in the groin."

"We were awesome," Pudge said, giving the twins high-fives.

"Did you see those pirates run?" Flim squeaked, she was so excited.

"They ran, huh?" Midge prompted.

"More like fell," Flam said.

"On top of each other," Flim added, giggling.

"We wewe weally scawy," Thumb said.

Zonk's smile nearly cracked her face. It was clear how happy she was to see and hear Thumb full of life. "You were," she said. "Really scary." She looked at Piper.

Here it comes, Piper thought. She's going to lay into me for the danger I put them all in. She hunched her shoulders and shoved her hands into her pockets.

"Weren't they, Pan?" Zonk pressed.

"Huh?" Why was Zonk calling her Pan? "Oh—yeah," Piper said. "Super scary. Fabulous job, all of you," she said, looking around at the group. "I don't know where to start—to thank you, that is. For saving me."

"You saved Thumb," Zonk pointed out.

"No," Piper said. She couldn't keep the bitter edge out of her voice. "I saved Belle. She saved Thumb."

"Same thing, right?" Zonk asked.

Piper shrugged.

The fairy stayed quiet.

Everyone looked from Piper to Belle and back. Shoot, Piper thought, what am I going to tell them? They're grateful to Belle, and Stinky adores her. Now's not the time to tell them all about the fairy and Captain Li'l Jack. But the girls just looked back and forth between them. Clearly they had better sense than to ask what had happened.

Piper shifted from one foot to the other. Her hands fiddled, restless. "You saved my life. All of you. Thank you." Her voice sounded as awkward as she felt.

"Sure thing," Pudge said. "So ... it'll be okay if we save the pirates, too, right?"

Everyone laughed. The request took Piper off guard. She managed a weak smile.

"It's just that we don't want them to starve," Pudge confessed. "The other pirates will never come looking for them in this part of the woods. They think it's haunted."

"She's right," Midge said. She tilted her head the way she did when she was cooking up something clever. "Zonk, where's the dugout?" Midge asked.

Zonk pointed ahead and to the left. "That way— just at the top of the beach."

"Good," Midge said. "I've got an idea."

They'd taken only a few steps toward the beach, when something changed. The moon disappeared, and the air thrummed like distant thunder. Piper's heart dropped into her stomach. She knew what it was immediately. This was an enemy she was powerless to fight. The other girls ducked instinctively, and no wonder. It seemed like the sky was about to crush them.

Zonk turned her head and stared. "What is it?"

"Sincoraz." Piper barely breathed the name, but it brought whimpers from Stinky and the twins.

She heard teeth chattering, from the direction of the pirate captives. They were literally quaking in their boots. One of them was muttering something that sounded like a prayer. Another started to cry.

Piper had seen the dragon before, but still she struggled to comprehend the giant airborne beast. Those were its wings, blocking the moon and slicing the air. It was too enormous, too terrible to be real.

But the hairs standing erect on the back of her neck, and the shudder rippling down her spine told her otherwise.

"It's headed to the ship," Piper said. "Everyone— we've got to get out of here, *now*."

"No way am I moving until I'm sure I'm safe from that thing." Pudge's whisper was as loud as a whisper could be and still qualify.

"She's right," Zonk said. "We should stay hidden. Come on, we'll crawl to the beach. We can watch from there."

"I'm not sure I want to," Midge said.

Piper didn't say it aloud, but she agreed with Midge.

†

"C-c-cap'n!" Flea's voice squeaked above the hammering and thumping of the crew.

Captain Li'l Jack ignored him, instead delivering threats to the men unlucky enough to be nearby. They worked haphazardly, their movements frenzied, following his orders to repair the ship. It was dark. He knew it was the wrong time, but he'd rather walk the plank than let that Pan girl defeat him! She wouldn't get far, in the state she'd been in. As long as the ship could sail, he could find her tomorrow, when daylight returned.

"Cap'n!" Flea's voice came again, without the stutter, but even higher. "Pardon me, Captain, Sir, but did ye set the red lanterns aloft?"

"What do ye mean, Flea?" the captain bellowed, glancing toward the crow's nest. "Of course I didn't—"

The sight that met his eyes took the life from his words like a desert sun bleaching bones. Two red orbs shone above the ship. But not two red lanterns. Those were far too large to be lanterns. Those spinning red orbs were hungry dragon eyes. Sincoraz's eyes.

A voice came to him, like wind, thunder, and rain combined. "It … is … time."

"Time for what?" Captain Li'l Jack asked, hoping to buy a few moments to compose himself.

"Time … to … feast." Sincoraz hung in the air, wings beating a rhythm of doom.

Pirates panicked. Some ran below deck, a few jumped overboard. Surely an avenging sea spirit would be gentler than the monster drooling above them. Li'l Jack fought his own instinct to flee. He had no cause to be afraid, he told himself. He was the Dragon Keeper. The beast could only feast when he gave it food. It was up to him to lay down the rules.

"Not tonight, my dear dragon." The power and authority in his voice surprised him. He was amazed he could summon such cool command under the circumstances. But why be amazed? He was the Scourge of the Seven Seas! "Tonight, we repair our ship." He tried for a tone of conciliation. "Tomorrow we shall hunt."

"Hungry ... now," the beast insisted, its voice slicing the air.

The captain had a brilliant idea. "Well then, I have the perfect morsel for you. There is a succulent yet satisfying mouthful, not far from here. Peter Pan's heir." The thought of the dragon inhaling that child made his blood run hot, and his voice quicken. "It's a girl—I presume she will taste exceptionally sweet."

"Not ... ripe," the dragon griped.

"If ye must stand on principle, then ye'll have to wait for tomorrow's foray. But if ye 're that hungry, find the girl! Now go! Back to your lair!"

Sincoraz's wing-beats sent vibrations through the sails, the masts, and the ship's deck. There wasn't a soul on board who wasn't quaking, too, including the captain.

"Go, I say!" Fear made his voice sharp. "And don't return until I summon ye properly!"

The fell beast hissed, and the water around the *Jolly Roger* steamed. Then its wings flexed, drawing the dragon backwards. It circled the cove, once, twice, a third time—and seemed to hover over the beach. Then it screamed, a sound like fingernails on a chalkboard. Wings beating, it rose higher and flew inland, back toward the den of its own making, the crater in the mountains.

The pirates cheered. The captain let out the breath he'd been holding. For now, they were safe. And he would have time, tomorrow, to find and finish off the girl, assuming the dragon didn't do it for him first. After that he'd gladly go hunting. He only required one or two more forays, after all, to have enough Elixir collected. Enough Life Elixir to make his dream come true. Real hands! The thrill of excitement drove his attention back to the present.

"Back to work, ye bleedin' blighters! I want this craft ship-shape before dawn!"

†

Piper watched Sincoraz make its third pass over the cove, and prayed that it would just go away. But then it seemed to see them, huddled at the edge of the beach, and it paused, its wings making a *whump, whump* sound. She wanted to cover her head and her ears with her arms. She would have given anything to just disappear. But the others were here. If it was here to snack, as the captain had suggested, it was looking for her.

Trembling, she rose to her feet, and walked a few paces away from the others. It was foolish to think she could lead it away, but that was exactly what she wanted to do. A memory flew into her head, of a mother bird, hopping along with an apparently broken wing, making noise to beat the band, just to keep her away from its nest of babies. Noise wasn't an option—it would draw the pirates—but movement was.

Backing into the trees, she waved her arms over her head. She had its attention, no doubt about that. Its whirling red eyes made her so afraid she thought she might pee her pants, then and there. She waited, expecting its mouth to open, the inhalation that would consume her to begin. But it just hovered there. *Whump, whump, whump.*

Go ahead, Sincoraz! Piper sent her thoughts with a force equal to yelling. *Eat me now and get it over with! Just leave the others alone!*

A noise split the air, sending actual shooting pain down her spine, and she fell to her knees. The dragon screamed. Still, she met its gaze, defiant.

Its enormous body moved through the air with the ease of a fish in water.

Whump, whump, whump. The wings beat harder, and the dragon pulled back and up. Its enormous body moved through the air with the ease of a fish in water. Higher and higher it rose, then it flew inland.

Piper threw up before wobbling back to the others. "C'mon, guys," she said. "Midge, lead the way."

CHAPTER TWENTY-TWO

Reviewing the Situation

Midnight had come and gone by the time the girls slid into the Underground Home. Piper didn't think she'd ever felt so tired. Midge had been eager to mastermind what to do with the pirates, Belle had seemed happy to help, and Piper had just kept a low and quiet profile.

They returned from Kidd's Cove via air in the dugout, courtesy of Belle's slim supply of pixie dust, after first searching out a small valley where they left off their prisoners. Belle said the place was called "Slightly Gulch." Leaving the men laying on the ground, the girls agreed it was better than in the brambles of a "haunted" wood.

They stopped to wash off the mud near home—so they were more or less clean. But they were damp, bedraggled, chilly and very tired.

"Do you think we could risk having a fire tonight?" Stinky stood shivering by the empty fireplace. She looked hopefully at Piper. "We can put it out before we fall asleep," she coaxed.

Piper had forbidden indoor fires since the girls

had arrived, to avoid risk of sending their home up in flames. After all, the Never Tree grew only feet away from the hearth. But she didn't want to call the shots just now. She felt she had lost that privilege. She looked at Zonk, who looked at Midge, who shrugged.

"I guess just this once we could do it." The strain of the day showed on Midge's face. "The pirates will stay on the *Jolly Roger* tonight for sure, so they won't see the smoke."

"I don't think we're safe here at all," Piper blurted, unable to help herself. "When the pirates look for me tomorrow, this is where they'll look first."

"You'll have to move," Belle said from her corner, "but not tonight."

"Right, but before dawn tomorrow, we'll have to get out of here. Belle, I want you—"

"Don't you think you ought to keep a lookout tonight?" Belle cut Piper off, her tone sharp.

"Huh?" Piper took a step back, confused.

"I'll do it," Zonk volunteered.

Pip recovered, and put a hand on Zonk's arm. "I know you would, Zonk, but if any of you are out there, I won't sleep. So it has to be me." Before turning to climb out, she whispered, "I know what you had to do tonight, and I'm sorry. Thank you for your courage."

Zonk felt a flush of warmth spreading outward from her heart. Pan knew about her having to stab the pirate. She felt better even before getting warm and fed.

"We'll go get firewood." Flim and Flam wiggled outside, in Pan's wake. Within moments pinecones and sticks of various sizes started dropping down their hollow tree.

"Are you feeling any better?" Stinky knelt beside Belle.

Zonk watched, eyes narrowed. Everyone but Pan had insisted on bringing the fairy home with them for the night. The hung-over pixie had taken up her old place of residence: a rounded hollow in the Underground Home outfitted just for her. She seemed a little put out by it, though. Probably it made her miss Peter.

"We saw your digs," Zonk said.

Belle stared, uncomprehending.

"I mean the place you live. Your fairy castle," Zonk explained. "The one on the bank of Mysterious River."

Belle looked away, straightening her very rumpled feather dress.

"Maybe you have others," Zonk finished.

Belle shook her head. "No, that's Faery's Nook," she said. "I've lived there a long time now." She hesitated, as if to say more, but didn't.

"It's pwetty," Thumb said. The little one lay curled in a blanketed basket.

"Thank you." Belle smiled a little. "Do you know who used to sleep in that basket?"

"Mmm-hmmm," Thumb nodded. "Michael used to sleep hewe."

"How did you know?" Belle looked puzzled.

"We all know," Pudge said. "*Peter Pan* was one of the DVDs we had at the foster home. We've all seen it dozens of times."

"DVDs?" Belle's eyes glazed and her wings drooped.

"Never mind," Zonk said. She still felt suspicious of Belle, even though the fairy had told them all about the fake dinner invitation from Captain Li'l Jack and her unwilling imprisonment. Midge had described the remains of a very fancy dinner in the captain's quarters. That was no fake dinner invitation. There was something the fairy wasn't telling them. Pan seemed to know, but she wasn't talking either.

"I miss movie night," Thumb mumbled, her namesake firmly in her mouth.

"We could tell stories," Stinky said, looking

around uncertainly. "I bet Belle has lots of them." She sighed dreamily.

"Is that enough?" Flim's head appeared from above, upside-down.

"Huh?" Zonk blinked at the pile of firewood spread across the floor. She hadn't been paying any attention to it. "Oh. Yeah."

With the fire blazing, everyone huddled around it except Thumb, who was already asleep, Belle, who stayed in her fairy corner, and Pan, who insisted on keeping her lookout post outside in the tree's branches. In spite of the relaxing warmth and the comfort of being home again, tension clung like an unwanted guest.

"Pan's in a weird mood," Midge said. "Do you think she's gonna be okay?"

Zonk shrugged. "Sure she will." She looked around at the other five worried faces. Trying to lighten things up, she added, "She's tough as nails, just like the rest of us."

"I wonder if she's sad," Flam said.

"Sad? About what?" Zonk asked, surprised.

"About her parents," Flim explained. "We've all known our parents are gone for a long time. She just found out a few days ago."

Silence stretched on as they pondered this, staring into the crackling flames.

"She's prob'ly lonely," Pudge said.

"She's prob'ly cold," Stinky added, moving closer to the fire.

"Maybe she's embarrassed about having to be saved," Midge reasoned. "But we're all cool with that, right?"

"Of course!"

"Sure we are!"

"Why wouldn't we be?"

"It was a blast!"

"Even if it was scary," Zonk said.

"Right," Midge agreed. "I bet she has some kind of plan."

You can count on Midge to be the practical voice, Zonk thought. Somehow that comforted her.

"What we have to do now," Midge continued, "is find out what that plan is, so we can help."

"Hope she doesn't do something stupid," Pudge muttered.

"Like what?" Zonk poked the fire with a stick, turning a log. Sparks showered up the chimney.

"I dunno." Pudge picked at the frayed edge of her pajama bottoms. She didn't meet anyone's eyes. She finally looked up, eyes bleak. "What if she goes and feeds herself to the dragon or something?"

"Nah," Midge said. "She won't do that. She might

do something idiotic, like take on the whole pirate crew in a swordfight, but not the dragon thing."

"How come not?" Flam nestled closer to her twin.

"Because she's got us now," Midge answered, simply. "I have a theory." She sat up on her knees and folded her hands in her lap. "I think she *planned* to fly off to the Neverland."

"What d' ya mean?" Pudge scoffed. "She didn't know she was related to Peter Pan until Belle brought her here. She told us so."

"True," Midge agreed. "She didn't know yet that she's Piper Pan. But remember she kept getting caught trying to jump from high places?" She shook her head, frowning. "She must've been trying to get to the Neverland."

"Mmmm," Pudge commented. "So she wasn't just loony-tunes." She laughed.

Zonk smiled. "Makes sense."

"What if she hadn't got caught?" Pudge asked.

"She would've hurt herself," Midge said, her face solemn. "I don't think she could've flown without Belle."

"For sure," Zonk said. "She still can't fly without help. At least that's what she said."

"Right." Belle's voice came from her corner.

They all turned and looked at the rumpled fairy.

"Will you teach us to fly?" Stinky asked, her eyes shining.

"I certainly will." Belle fluffed her hair. "Tomorrow, first thing." She lay down and closed her eyes as if she hadn't a care in the world.

Zonk exchanged glances with Midge and Pudge. Their faces reflected the reservations she felt.

"It'll be a start," Midge said. "Whatever Pan's plan is, we'll need to be mobile. Flying on our own would be more efficient than flying around in the dugout, and we could break into teams if we need to. That could be a real advantage."

Zonk saw the gleam in Midge's eyes, as the wheels in her clever head started turning. She nodded. "Let's keep the flying boat a secret."

"The prisoners already know about it," Flim protested.

"Yeah, but they'll think they were seeing things," Midge said.

"Oh. Like they were under our spell?" Flam giggled.

"By the time we get a note to the captain telling him where to find them," Midge continued, "They'll be so whacked out no one will believe anything they say anyway. Who would think they were really passengers in a flying dugout canoe?"

"It takes too much pixie dust for me to keep

flying that boat." Belle lay facing away from them, but her voice reached them easily.

So much for her being asleep over there. Zonk rolled her eyes.

"Stop it," Stinky said, elbowing Zonk in the ribs.

"No." Zonk poked her back.

Far from being asleep, Belle sat up and came to the entry of her alcove. "I'm going out to keep Piper company. You should get to sleep. You'll need your rest for learning to fly." With her chin up, the fairy did an ungainly takeoff and made her exit, flying in a wobbling pattern.

"Okay, everybody," Midge directed. "Belle is right. It's lights-out time. Tomorrow will be a big day. We've got to learn to fly, figure out a safe place to relocate our camp, and move forward with Pan's plan, whatever it is."

Zonk helped Midge tuck in Stinky and the twins, and Pudge put out the fire before they each crawled into their hammocks. Several minutes passed. Pudge started to snore.

"Zonk?" Midge said quietly.

"Yeah?"

"Do you miss Seattle?"

Zonk counted three breaths before answering. "No."

"Me neither."

Zonk smiled in the dark.

From her lookout post in the branches of the Hollow Tree, Piper saw Belle flying toward her. The little old fairy landed in a heap on a wide branch beside her. But Piper didn't look at her. Not straight on. She was still too angry. No—not so much angry—really, she was too hurt. How could Belle have sold her out to the pirate captain that way?

They sat in silence for a time, listening to the girls wishing each other good night in the Underground Home below. When the voices fell silent, a lone cricket's chirp filled the space between them.

Piper thought the air smelled a little like sulfur, which kept her heart in her throat. The pirates were a terrible threat, but the dragon was way beyond that. The dragon was unbeatable. When Sincoraz's whirling red eyes had stared into hers, Piper had been sure it was all over. She shuddered, remembering. What would she do if it showed up here, hanging in the sky over the Never Tree, hungry and terrifying?

"It's just the smell of the fire downstairs going out," Belle said.

"What are you, a mind reader?" Piper snapped.

She hadn't meant to speak so sharply, but then again, maybe she had.

"Sometimes, that's exactly what I am." Belle fluttered to a tiny branch closer to Piper's eye level.

The better to confront you, my dear, Piper thought. But what she said aloud was "Oh?"

"Yes. 'Oh.' I know perfectly well you want me to take you all back to Seattle."

Piper just stared. That was exactly what she wanted.

"It's the next thing you want me to do to repay you for saving my life," Belle explained. "And we needed to talk about that away from the others."

"That's why you sent me out here," Piper said, the realization popping in her head like a soap bubble.

"Right." Belle wrapped her arms around her ribcage.

Piper wondered if this feathered fairy was cold, or feeling something else. Afraid? Defensive? Well, she should feel defensive, Piper thought, with a bite.

Belle sighed. "Look. There are two things. First, I don't have anywhere near the supply of pixie dust we would need to fly the dugout all the way back to Seattle. Not yet. I'll need several days to recover before I'll have it."

"Fine," Piper snapped. "Then we need a plan for where to hide for those several days."

"Second," Belle hissed, her teeth exposed in a cat-like growl, "Seattle is the first place Captain Li'l Jack will look for you, if he doesn't find you here in the Neverland—"

Piper opened her mouth to interrupt, but Belle stopped her with a warning finger.

"—and I know that you want, above all, to keep the other girls safe."

Piper's mouth stayed open, this time in surprise.

"If he goes to Seattle, he won't just find you. He'll find all of them."

"Not if I just drop them off and run away!" Piper said, defiant.

"Why would you do that?" Belle asked. "You've finally made friends. You're connected now. They're your—what did you call it? Your 'Merry Band.'"

Piper let that sink in.

"You think so?" She hadn't meant to ask.

"Of course. Thanks to you, they just did something that made them prouder of themselves than they've ever been."

"But I failed as their leader!" Piper said.

"How did you fail? You helped them gain skills and confidence in themselves. What more should a leader do?"

"A leader should not get captured and force everyone to save her."

"Slug trails and snail slime!" Belle's wings vibrated irritation. "Look, Piper Pan. You showed bravery and loyalty. You were willing to sacrifice yourself to keep the other girls safe. And you risked your life to save me."

Piper looked at her hands in her lap. "To save Thumb," she corrected.

"Right," said Belle, her voice crisp. "My point is you behaved like a hero. But that isn't why they're willing to follow you anywhere. They'll do *that* because you love them."

"You're saying all it takes to make friends is to love someone?"

"Most of the time, yes. Showing that you care is powerful magic."

Piper was quiet for a moment, listening to the cricket chirp. Belle was saying the others wanted her. A bright thrill shimmered through her. *Real friends.* Think how wonderful life could be, she thought, with real friends! It would almost be like belonging.

"You have a place, Piper Pan," Belle continued. "Whether you are ready to own it or not, the Neverland is your place. Being Piper Pan is your purpose in life. Why would you abandon that?"

Tears welled in Piper's eyes. Belle was right. More than anyplace she'd been since her parents had disappeared from their happy family apartment near the Space Needle, the Neverland felt like home. Even though the place was cursed and nearly lifeless. She met Belle's eyes straight on. "I'm sorry I couldn't save it for you."

"It's not too late," Belle said, eyebrows raised in a challenge.

Piper ignored it. She had enough to worry about without trying to fly again. Instead, she shook her head in wonder at Belle's insight. She *did* belong here—at least she did now that her parents were never coming back.

And with *friends*, Piper's thought continued, with *real friends*, it would be so much better! Who cared about bare trees and dry earth? As long as they had the honeyed spring water, and a safe place to live, the whole island could be their playground! Who knew, maybe they could all learn to fly. And they could definitely play pirate—

The pirates. Piper's face fell. Having friends didn't diminish the danger they were in from Captain Li'l Jack and his crew. There wasn't any place safe from the pirates in the Neverland. Maybe there wasn't a place *anywhere* they'd be safe.

If she'd learned one thing in the last terrifying day, it was to keep those who are precious to you, safe. The best chance the girls had now was to be far away from her. The irony of it made Piper's throat ache. It seemed her love only put people in danger. First her parents, now her friends.

"I see you understand," Belle said, misinterpreting Piper's expression completely. "So what we need to do, is to find a protected place here in the Neverland for you and your Merry Band. We need all of you to learn to fly, and then we can go about the business of bringing the Neverland back to life."

"Oh no you don't." Piper's tone made it clear Belle was not welcome to continue with that line of thought. "You *are* right that I want them safe. And you *are* right, actually, that I belong in the Neverland," she admitted. "What you *aren't* right about, is that they should stay here and risk their lives with me."

"But—"

"This time it's my turn to talk," Piper said. "In a few minutes, I'm going to take a catnap while you keep a lookout, if you really think it'll do any good, and then I'm going to take my things and go."

"But where will you go?"

"What do you care?" Piper regretted the verbal jab when she saw the look on Belle's face. For whatever reason, in her strange fairy way, clearly Belle did care. Piper cleared her throat, wanting to dislodge the sudden lump of shame. "Don't worry about me. I'll be fine. I just have to stay one step ahead of the pirates, and I can do that."

Belle looked doubtful.

Piper went back to giving directions. "Tomorrow, get the girls up and going as soon as there's light. Take them somewhere safe on the island. You know the Neverland like the back of your hand. Can you think of someplace safe?"

The fairy nodded. "There's a cave in Mermaid's Lagoon the pirates don't know about."

"Good," Piper said. She felt a weight lift from her chest. "Go ahead and teach them to fly," she coaxed. "They'll love it, I know they will. I'm sure they'll be better students than I was."

Belle looked relieved.

"But as soon as the flying lessons are done, I expect you to take them all back to Seattle."

"Back to that awful place?" From Belle's expression, she must be thinking about horrid Mrs. Fitch.

Piper snorted. "Yes. At least they won't be in danger of being drowned, stabbed, burned, or whatever other nasty punishments the pirates can think of."

Belle seemed reluctant, but eventually nodded.

"If they can all fly," Piper reasoned, "you'll be able to leave right away instead of waiting for enough pixie dust for the dugout."

"I'll need enough to fly myself," Belle insisted.

"No you won't," Piper said. "If the others can fly, they can carry you. Stinky would be thrilled to do that, I'm sure. And you can still tell everyone where to go."

"Ha." Belle looked put out, but had no other comment.

"All righty then," Piper said. "We're straight, right? You promise to take them back?"

Belle tightened her lips, but agreed. "I promise."

Piper nodded. She still wasn't easy with Belle. She didn't know where they stood, and was afraid to ask. But she believed the little old fairy would keep her word. "Thank you," she said, "for saving Thumb."

"You're welcome," Belle answered.

Satisfied, Piper propped herself in the crook of the Never Tree. She'd no more than closed her eyes, when exhaustion overtook her and she slid into sleep.

She'd hoped to spend a dreamless hour or two, but the vision of a hungry dragon, eyes whirling red, wouldn't leave her in peace.

Belle watched her small charge sleep. She, too, was exhausted, but uneasy thoughts kept her from relaxing. She'd given her word to do everything she could to keep the girls out of harm's way. But what about the Neverland? She couldn't just let that go. In spite of her inability to fly, laugh, or crow, Belle still needed Piper to save her precious home. She'd seen Piper fight. She'd experienced her heart. The girl seemed more like Peter's granddaughter every day.

Could she really just give in and let Piper throw away her life fighting Li'l Jack and his men? Belle sighed. She'd lost Li'l Jack tonight. It was crystal clear that there would be no going back to getting her way through the handsome pirate captain. She'd lost sway over him. This betrayal of his was his last, because she would not give him another opportunity.

Yes, she'd lost Captain Li'l Jack. Now, it looked like she was about to lose Peter's granddaughter as well. And with her, all hope of breaking the curse of the Neverland.

Belle shook her head in frustration, and buried her face in her hands. She'd known getting herself involved with a bunch of girls would be trouble. Spreading her fingers, she peered between them, and watched Piper's face, twitching in dreams. Too late now. Too late to get uninvolved, too late to undo what had been done. Piper Pan was here in the Neverland, and with her, a whole pack of trouble.

Belle took a deep breath and faced the truth. She hadn't bargained for this. She hadn't bargained for the ache in her heart. She'd fallen hard for this Trouble, this Piper Pan.

Royal Reflections

It was teatime, once again, in the palace sunroom. Sunbeams poured through beveled glass panes, and rainbows danced on the white linen tablecloth.

King Oberon set his empty teacup on its saucer, and leaned back, hands clasped behind his head. A teacake crumb clung to the corner of his mouth. He whistled a tune, and the tips of his royal wings twitched in accompaniment.

Queen Titania looked up from the *Crystal City Daily News* and inspected her husband. One perfectly arched eyebrow quirked up, mirroring her half-smile.

"Surely, you do not expect me to break into a chorus of 'Into the West.'"

"*Au contraire.*" The king leaned forward, resting his elbows on the table.

"Tsk, tsk, tsk," the queen chided, nose back in her newspaper. "Manners, darling."

"A Hallelujah chorus will be fine," the king continued, not budging his elbows. He reached for another teacake and broke it in half. Crumbs littered white linen. He handed half to his queen.

Queen Titania folded the newspaper and laid it aside. She accepted his offering, setting it neatly on its proper plate. She picked up her teacup and regarded the king as she sipped. The amused expression on her face had turned serious.

"Progress is being made, 'tis true, my king," she said, her tone gentle.

"Progress? We've come miles from where we began," Oberon insisted. "Hearts are opening. Forgiveness is nigh. The path of true service beckons them all." He bit into his teacake, talking around his mouthful. "Clever minds whirl with ideas galore!"

"Ideas are what got them in this mess," Titania said.

"Ideas, no! 'Twas loneliness at fault!" The king's passion for his subject fueled his gestures, ever grander.

"A compassionate spin," Titania said. "I would say this—greed and vanity, also selfishness." She reached for the china teapot, wrapped in a tea cozy emblazoned with a smiley face and the injunction to *Have a Nice Day!*

Teacups refilled, she sighed. "Sweetheart, I would spare you disappointment, in case the girl's unable to come through. Clever minds are at work. But one, at least, still operates on the basis of greed."

"But—"

"Hearts *are* op'ning," Queen Titania continued, holding a finger up to silence the king, "but they're not yet whole. As to walking the path of true service—we've seen selfish, next we'll see servitude. That is not what comprises true service. You know it as well as I do, my king."

"My dear," the king insisted, "you simply must practice your faith!"

"In humans?" The queen's tone left no doubt as to her feeling about that.

"You underestimate them," the king said. "Look at we fairies. Humans hold our hearts. Why else do you think we emulate them? You know the law that Parliament passed—forbidding flying in the Crystal City? If their human will never reclaim them, our fairies will strive to *become* human!"

The queen waved the insights away. "This is not the time for philosophy. The Neverland still faces immense odds. It may fall from the magical kingdom. Consider, my dear, the dragon alone. Can it return to its proper design? The Neverland is still perched on the brink. It needs a miracle to revive it," she finished.

"Ah, my queen, but that is where we come in,"

the king winked, wiping crumbs from his mouth with one hand.

"We aren't in the business of miracles." The queen's voice was sharp.

The king reached to take her hand in both of his. "No. We are in the business of magic. That certainly counts for something, my queen. And as for the business of miracles, the Neverland can access them as well."

The queen's face softened. "I hope you are correct, I truly do."

"Never stop believing. Faith brings magic." The king smiled—a contagious thing.

The queen followed suit. "We'll just have to wait and see, won't we, dear?" She patted his hands with her free one. "But do not forget the laws of free will."

"I recall free will," the king promised. He watched her return to her reading. "I'm counting on it," he said to himself. He leaned back and whistled the Hallelujah chorus.

THE END OF BOOK ONE

Would you like to download free character posters? Visit
www.PiperPanAndHerMerryBand.com *and join*
Piper's Merry Band to gain access.

If you've enjoyed this book, please consider leaving an
honest review on Amazon or goodreads.com

If you are an introspective adult reader, you might relish
using the Reading Guide for Inner Reflection as
a journaling tool. Download it at
www.piperpanandhermerryband.com/resources

SOME THINGS TO THINK AND TALK ABOUT

Classroom discussion questions and activities follow.

1. Personal Values are qualities a person judges to be most important in their life—a person's principles, or standards of behavior. Name four of Piper's values. Does she honor these values at all times, or just sometimes? Do you think it's important for a person to have a set of values? Why or why not?

2. Any value has extremes—too little and too much as well as just right. When you understand the examples, fill in the blanks for the other values. Note: there can be more than one right answer, and you can use more than one word.

Examples:

Just Right	Too Little	Too Much
Courage	Cowardice	Foolhardiness
Compassion	Indifference	Indulgence
Loyalty	_____	_____
Trust	_____	_____
Persistence	_____	_____

Give examples of these qualities as demonstrated by the characters in the book.

3. At the beginning of the book, Piper decides to take the ultimate risk to try to get to the Neverland to save her parents: she tries to "fly" off of a bridge. Do you think this was a good plan? Why or why not? What could she have done differently? If someone you know is talking about doing something dangerous, what can you do to help them see options, or to connect them with someone who can help?

4. When Piper arrives at Fitch's Last Ditch Foster Home, the Lifers aren't very welcoming. Not only do they mistrust Piper, they don't seem to be treating each other like friends. Why would a group of outsiders, or misfits, not be bonded together? What does it take for the Lifers to bond—to become the Merry Band?

5. When Captain Li'l Jack is being rowed ashore to watch Piper drown at high tide, he remembers his own childhood and tries not to dwell on the way Piper reminds him of himself at the same age. Did it change the way you felt about Captain Li'l Jack to know how and why he came to the Neverland? Why or why not?

6. What would you say Piper thinks of Belle after the two of them bring the girls from Fitch's Last Ditch Foster Home to the Neverland? Why is Piper so shocked when she sees Belle on board the *Jolly Roger* "caged" in the captain's quarters? At the end of the book, Piper still hasn't completely forgiven Belle. What do you think of that? Should she be more forgiving? Less? Why?

7. After Piper has been captured, the girls need a leader. Who do they turn to and why? Pudge is the oldest, why don't they turn to her? What does Midge have to overcome to be the one to decide on the rescue plan?

8. Why does Zonk appoint herself to the task of freeing Piper from the pier? What do you imagine it takes for Zonk to do whatever is needed to make it happen? How do you think she feels about having to kill the pirate?

9. Friendship is an important theme in the Piper Pan and Her Merry Band book series. What qualities make for a good friend? If you had to choose just one of the girls as a friend, which one would you choose, and why?

10. At the beginning of the book, Pudge is kind of a bully to Piper. If someone is being mean to you or someone else, what can you do about it? Come up with several choices along with pros and cons for each choice.

11. Talk about ways friends help each other. What things make being friends hard? What things aren't OK between friends? If someone doesn't have any friends like Piper in the beginning of the book, what are some ways they might make friends?

12. In the world of the book, it's clear that every child is born with a personal fairy. Whether or not that's true, has there ever been a time in your life, or in the life of someone you know, when you (or they) got help and it felt amazing, almost magical, to get that help?

13. What are five ways you think using your imagination can make your life better, or happier, or more fun?

ACTIVITIES TO CHOOSE FROM

Make believe you've been transported to the Neverland, and like Piper, you find it nearly dead. Write a page about what you would do while you are there.

- Dress up as your favorite character from the book.

- Imagine what it was like for Captain Li'l Jack when he first arrived in the Neverland; when he decided he didn't want to be a Lost Boy and was delivered to the *Jolly Roger* as a cabin boy. Write a story about one of his adventures.

- Use art supplies to portray a character (or characters): draw, paint, collage, sculpt—the sky's the limit!

- Play "let's make believe." Spend the day (or an hour) as a pirate or a fairy: dress up, talk in character, give yourself a name, talk with each other and see what happens.

- In your mind, take yourself to the first days in the Neverland with Piper and the Lifers. The book "fast forwards" through those days of struggle and training. Write a short story about something that might have happened during those days before Piper was captured.

- Draw your version of what kind of space you would want to stay in, in the Neverland. Would it be a treehouse? Something underground? A cave? On the beach? In the forest?

AN INTERVIEW WITH THE AUTHOR

Have you always wanted to be a writer?

When I was 10 years old, the list of what I wanted to be when I grew up went something like this: actor, artist, singer, dancer, musician, performer, writer and gardener. While writing was on the list, it wasn't until I hit 40 years old and closed the door on my professional acting dreams that I seriously began to write. I had written in a journal for years, but never thought I had what it takes to be a good storyteller. I'm proof that it's a learnable skill, one that I hope to grow.

Are you a reader?

I've always been an avid reader. My father read aloud to my brothers and me almost every evening as we grew up. It's a treasured and hugely impactful memory. I consume stories (books, movies, audios) today as if they were chocolate: that is to say, in great quantities and with delight.

With all the Peter Pan and Neverland spin-offs, why create this one?

I played Peter Pan on stage when I was 11 years old. In retrospect it was a foundational visceral experience for me, of freedom, power, and joy. The irony was that I was pretending to be a boy to have that experience. With this series I've had the chance to take my memories of the Neverland and recreate them with girls front and center. I'd like the Neverland to give other girls the same freedom, power, and joy it gave me.

Who did you write the book for?

To be perfectly honest, I wrote it for myself. It's the experience I would have wanted to have if I could have gone to the Neverland. It's an adventure with important emotional stakes—with characters striving toward meaningful change. I find some of my biggest fans are other women who remember J.M. Barrie's rules that Neverland was only for girls once a year, at Spring Cleaning. I suppose knowing those original rules adds to the pleasure of discovering the new ones in my book. Women readers over 50 also have an innate appreciation for Belle.

You live in the Pacific Northwest—is that why the book starts in Seattle?

Yes. When choosing a setting, writing about what you know is a practical place to start. Also, Seattle is a vibrant theater town, so Piper's parents could have lived and worked there, on Queen Anne, close to the Space Needle.

Are there other things from your life that found their way into the book?

Of course. It's hard to write about anything without it holding clues about yourself. But speaking specifically: I moved a lot while growing up, and understand the experience of being an "oddball" like the Lifers. Friendship was and still is something I hold extremely dear. I've come to believe in fairies as an adult, and I'd love for young people to retain their imagination, sense of wonder and possibility rather than giving it up in the interest of growing up. And trees are some of my favorite beings in the world.

What do you hope people will take away from reading the book?

First, I'd like people to take a new look at how they use imagination in their lives—to give themselves permission to turn it on full force. It's not always about escaping—it's just as often about creating new possibilities, new solutions. And second, I hope this series, like so many other wonderful books for kids, encourages people of all ages to trust and believe in who they and their friends really are. The power of friendship to help us grow into ourselves cannot be overrated.

ACKNOWLEDGEMENTS

While writing is in essence a solitary task, the creation of a book is rarely accomplished alone. Certainly not in this case. I have many to thank for the fact that Piper Pan and her Merry Band have finally emerged in print. For publishing help, options, considerations, expertise, encouragement, and loads of assistance, Kelly Lenihan and Celeste Bennett. For editorial assistance and eagle-eyed proofreading, thanks to Celeste Bennett and Kathy Dahlen. For illustrations, artist Aisha Zaleha Latip, for cover and character card design, Marjorie Schoelles. My mother, Lin McLaughlin Bruce, for believing in Piper unceasingly ever since she read my first draft. My other First Readers: Jeremy Cowie, Jean Cowie, Gordon Forbes, Perrilee Pizzini, Dana Miller, Barbara Altstaetter, Robert K., Rob M., and Scott Bruce. Special gratitude to the girls and boys who gave me their seal of approval: Tigerlilly, Julia Rose, and Maggie Bruce, Marie, Chris, and Karl Ranney. Thanks to Tamara Schneider and Jessicka Chamberlin for inspired advice, unswerving faith, and energetic facilitation. Perrilee Pizzini, for allowing me to adopt a version of her last name for Piper.

For glorious years on stage at the Northfield Arts Guild, including playing Peter Pan at 11 years old, I thank directors Bev Pierce and Myrna Johnson. For my deep love of stories, I thank my father, Robert K. Bruce for bringing home books and giving them life through reading aloud. Thanks to all the authors too numerous to name whose work has fed my soul and made a writer of me in spite of myself.

I began my fiction writing education under the generous umbrella of RWA where I got to look at what really goes on under the sleek hood of a well-written story. Thanks to my Eastside RWA Chapter—especially to my early critique group—(you know who you are)! I tip my hat to Nora Roberts for leading me down the box canyon of "Oh, this can't be that hard, look at how many she's written!" Thank goodness for my error; I'd never have begun if not for that mistaken belief.

Thanks also to the many who inspired me through the Western Washington Chapter of SCBWI. Special gratitude for early encouragement and critique from author Laini Taylor, whose Dreamdark books are among my favorite.

In recent years, thanks to all the spiritual and heart-centered entrepreneurs who have shared their journeys with me and opened an entire world of purpose-driven, inspired fulfillment along with marketing savvy. You have my heart-felt gratitude.

To my North Olympic Library System cohorts and colleagues: thanks for the patience, humor, unflagging support, book recommendations, and fellowship. Here's to being fellow geeks and connoisseurs of fictional worlds. If only "Accio Books" could take the place of shelving!

To my own Merry Bands, near and far—your friendship and bottomless hearts have renewed my spirit again and again.

To my dear husband, Ty Youngblood, thank you for your care and devotion—you've made my heart bloom. Everyone should be so lucky as to have such a beloved.

ABOUT THE AUTHOR

photo credit: Kay Kepley

Lindy MacLaine is a grown-up who still believes in fairies. She and her fitness-loving husband live outside Seattle, flanked by ancient forests and magical mountains, in the home of their two cats.

www.PiperPanAndHerMerryBand.com
www.facebook.com/LindyMacLaineBooks